The A-List

Also by Zoey Dean:

GIRLS ON FILM

BLONDE AMBITION

TALL COOL ONE

BACK IN BLACK

The A-List

by
Zoey Dean

LITTLE, BROWN AND COMPANY

New York ⁊ Boston

Little, Brown and Company
Time Warner Book Group
1271 Avenue of the Americas, New York, NY 10020
Visit our Web site at www.lb-teens.com

First Edition

 Produced by 17th Street Productions,
an Alloy company
151 West 26th Street, New York, NY 10001

Cover photography (foreground image) copyright
Ryan McVay/Getty Images
Cover photography (background image) copyright
Robert Landau/Corbis

ISBN 0-316-73435-7

10 9 8 7 6

CWO

Printed in the United States of America

For Lisa Hurley: The A-Plus List

When I'm good, I'm very good,
but when I'm bad I'm better.
—Mae West

Prologue

The moment Cynthia Baltres peed all over an eight-thousand-dollar Hermès Kelly handbag was the moment that Anna Cabot Percy decided to make Cynthia her best friend.

That had been thirteen years ago, during afternoon tea at the St. Regis Hotel in Manhattan. The two girls' mothers had dragged Anna and Cyn along to a planning session for a charity gala. Before she became Mrs. Alfred Baltres III, Cynthia's mom had been a real estate agent on Long Island. Desperate to prove herself the equal of Jane "To the Manner Born" Percy, she'd focused all her attention on arranging the fund-raiser and missed her daughter's crotch-grabbing, a signal that she needed a trip to the ladies' room.

Cynthia never did take well to being ignored. As Anna stared in disbelief, Cynthia had hopped off her chair, squatted above her mother's purse, and let 'er rip. Mrs. Baltres turned the same shade of red as her fur-trimmed Versace pantsuit, grasped her doused handbag like it was a long-dead carp, and yanked her daughter off to the loo.

Anna, who would have spontaneously combusted

before she'd ever urinate in public, had been very impressed. That her own mother, clad in vintage Chanel, continued to sip tea as a waiter mopped up didn't surprise Anna at all. At age five, she'd already learned her first lesson from the *This Is How We Do Things* Big Book, East Coast WASP edition: One simply didn't see what one did not choose to see.

There, in the storied tearoom of the St. Regis, little Anna had a vision of her destiny: She'd grow up to be just like her mother—perfectly genteel . . . and perfectly boring. The thought depressed her as much as a five-year-old with an eight-digit trust fund could be depressed. Life had to be more fun if you were shocking and bad. And if anyone could teach her those traits, it was Cynthia Baltres.

In the long run, though, genes had trumped desire, meaning that the friendship had taken but the badness hadn't. Thirteen years later, Anna had yet to do one truly nasty thing. She got excellent grades, preferred literature to movies, did charity work but rarely talked about it, and dated the right boys from the right families.

Sadly, though, the right boys from the right families had thus far generated about as much heat in Anna as Lady Chatterley's husband. But hope ("the thing with feathers," as her favorite poet, Emily Dickinson, so eloquently put it) still perched on her soul, singing within Anna's heart that someday the *wrong* boy would make her cry, "Don't stop!" and really mean it.

Ironically, Anna thought she already knew the boy: Scott Rowley. He'd moved to New York from Boston when he was fifteen, after his parents' divorce. Dad had gotten the Beacon Hill manse, the art collection, and the predictably nubile mistress. Mom had gotten the New York brownstone, the summer place on Block Island, and Scott.

Anna had loved Scott from the first moment she'd seen him leaning against a tree outside of Trinity, her school, reading *The Onion* and laughing aloud. But it soon became apparent that Anna's leggy, patrician blond beauty didn't register on Scott's sexual oscilloscope. He went for the exotic: a dreadlocked art student from Brazil, the black-hair-past-her-butt daughter of the Indonesian ambassador to the United Nations, a gorgeous five-foot-nine Ethiopian girl with a shaved head. The only thing that had eased the sting of Anna's unrequited love was her realization that Scott never hooked up with anyone born north of the equator.

That is, until three weeks ago, when he'd hooked up with her best friend, Cyn.

Though not traditionally beautiful, there was just something about Cyn. Men of all ages sniffed after her. Her mouth was thin and her nose had a slight bump in it, which she refused to "fix" since, she said, she was not "broken." Her hair was naturally dark brown, but she dyed it raven black and wore it in a choppy, sexy, messy style that drew attention to her startling celery-green eyes. Clothes hung perfectly on her skinny slim-hipped body. She could pull off styles that made other girls look ridiculous.

(Anna was well aware that Cynthia had, in fact, started

the trend of wearing boys' boxer shorts when she'd worn a pair to Paris Hilton's birthday party with a vintage CBGB T-shirt and red cowboy boots. By the next afternoon, it was nearly impossible to purchase a pair of guys' boxer shorts on the island of Manhattan.)

On top of that, Cynthia was up for anything. On a moment's notice she'd fly to Bora-Bora in some guy's private jet. Once she'd gone to the opera with her parents and spent the entire second act of *La Bohème* making out in the limo with a middle-aged man she'd met in the lobby—she never did get his name. Another time she'd gone to a party in SoHo where she'd pretended that she was French and ended up going home with a semi-famous painter who, after painting a nude of her, had threatened to kill himself if she wouldn't sleep with him. She hadn't, and he hadn't, but still. Anna loved to hear about Cyn's exploits; she got vicarious thrills without having to take any of the risks.

From Anna's point of view, Cyn really was All That. But even with her recently acquired rose tattoo midway between her navel and her pearly gates, Anna had been certain that Cyn was still not exotic enough for Scott. Anna had been wrong.

She'd meant to tell Cyn a thousand times that she loved Scott. But since Anna knew Scott would never love her back, divulging this seemed silly. And Anna Percy was not a silly girl.

Now it was too late.

Things had been going so well, too. Anna had been

accepted early decision to Yale. Her spring internship at a new literary journal meant she could fulfill her credits without having to take any more high school classes. Then, the day after Cyn-and-Scott had burst onto the scene, Anna's nineteen-year-old sister, Susan, had invited Anna to a party in a SoHo loft. Susan, who'd just broken up with her latest boyfriend, hated going to parties alone. She'd begged.

Anna had reluctantly agreed. At the party she'd been surprised to find herself actually having a decent time, chatting in the kitchen with a *Time Out: New York* photographer, when she realized she hadn't seen Susan in a while. She excused herself to look for her sister and found her passed out in the rooftop hot tub, naked except for a Randolph Duke mohair duster that floated around her like furry pond scum.

Anna gave Susan mouth-to-mouth, called 911, and saved her sister's life. But Susan didn't take well to Anna's methodology ("Could you have made any bigger of a scene out of it, Anna?"). Neither did Jane Percy, who shipped Susan back to rehab for the second time in a year and then took off for Italy to visit a twenty-eight-year-old sculptor whose work she was acquiring. She explained to Anna that remaining in New York would just be too trying. Besides, she was sure that Anna could fend for herself for a few weeks, what with two live-ins and a day staff of four to assist her.

Anna might have done it—stayed alone in Manhattan. But then she'd gotten word that there'd be no spring internship for her. The literary journal had burned through its start-up capital and folded after its second issue.

Jane had suggested that if Anna called her father in Los Angeles to tell him that she was going to Europe, he'd make a trip east. She was sure Susan would appreciate having her father visit her in rehab, especially since Susan's problems were an obvious result of said father's abandonment so many years ago. Anna agreed to inquire, all the while thinking that it was about as likely as McDonald's serving foie gras. She knew her father wouldn't come. She knew her mother knew it, too, but agreed to make the call because it was the right thing to do.

When the conversation proved fruitless ("I'd love to, Anna, honey, but I'm swamped with work"—exactly what she'd known he'd say), Anna had impetuously broached the idea of going out to Los Angeles to live with him. To her shock, her father had been enthusiastic about the idea. He'd even promised to arrange an internship with the Los Angeles office of a literary agency known for its prizewinning authors.

When, in the middle of that discussion, Cyn had beeped in on call waiting to regale Anna with a story about Scott's Frenching technique, Anna had had an epiphany: Maybe the reason Scott thought Cyn was sexy but didn't think that Anna was sexy was that Anna didn't think of *herself* as sexy. Certainly the reason she didn't have wild and crazy adventures like Cyn was that she never opened herself up to them. The horrible truth was that at not quite eighteen years of age, Anna had yet to step outside the box. She'd lived her entire life in the same safe and rarified confines as pretty much every other Upper East Side WASPy prep-school girl. As hard as she'd tried to fight it.

Anna's life didn't begin the rock slide to banality the day Cyn and Scott became Cyn-and-Scott; it had been rolling down that hill for a long time. Her life was boring and predictable, and it was her own fault.

Something had to be done about it. And she was the someone who had to do it. She could change. She *would* change. And not while hiding in the formidable shadow of Cynthia Baltres.

It was time for Anna Percy to "carpe diem," as her Latin teacher would say.

Seize the day.

One

"If you've got to do bumper-to-bumper, it's better in a Mercedes," Cyn told Anna, and took another long guzzle from the nearly empty bottle of Krug Clos du Mesnil champagne she'd purloined from her parents' wine cellar. The Percy family driver, Reginald, inched the car along the Van Wyck Expressway and pretended there weren't two underage girls drinking in the back-seat.

Cyn offered the bottle to Anna. "Go for it. We're still like a mile from JFK."

Anna shook her head. "No thanks." Her tongue felt thick and her lips were sticking to her teeth. "I think I had too much already."

"Bullshit. It's New Year's Eve."

"Actually, it's the morning of the day of New Year's Eve," Anna said, pleased that she could be so precise in her current condition.

"Out with the old, in with the new, huh?" Cyn threw her head back against the buttery leather. "Do you have any idea how bad life is going to suck without you?"

"I'm sure Scott will help you piss away the time." Anna popped a hand over her mouth. "I meant 'pass.' Pass away the time."

"Speaking of—tonight's the night. Scott Spencer will go where no man has gone before," Cyn said. There was an air of victory in her tone.

Anna was too good a friend to point out that in fact two guys *had* gone there before, because she knew that Cyn had been wasted on both occasions and had decided they didn't count. "I'm happy for you," she said, trying to mean it but failing miserably.

"I hate that I'm so into him. It's easier when you don't care."

Anna laughed. "They're going to stick your butt in the Smithsonian one of these days," Cyn remarked. "Anna Percy, world's oldest living virgin. Anyway, après Scott, I'll call and give you the blow by blow."

Though Anna could certainly learn a thing or two from the Cyn/Scott playback, she opted to spare herself the anguish. "You don't have to."

"Yes, I do. If I don't, it won't seem real. And I'll fly out to visit you soon."

"You'd better." Anna started to gather her things as Reginald slowed the car near the American Airlines terminal.

"Come on. Change your mind," Cyn begged. "If you think you'll be too lonely in your big-ass brownstone all by yourself, you can come live in our big-ass penthouse. There's plenty of room. One of the maids got deported."

For a moment Anna was tempted. Maybe she *was* making a mistake. Then she got a mental picture of Cyn making out with Scott in the hallway of Trinity or Cyn dancing on the bar at Hogs and Heifers (fake IDs came in so handy) while every guy in the place drooled over her. That was Cyn's New York life. Not Anna's. No. She was going.

Reginald pulled the black Mercedes to the curb, stepped out, and opened the door for the girls. They stood together on the sidewalk as hurried travelers pressed past. Cyn hugged Anna as hard as she could. "Don't let some jerk out there break your heart."

"I won't," Anna promised. Her heart had already been broken. And she planned to leave that broken heart far, far behind.

Anna sat in her first-class seat, staring out the window but seeing nothing, lost in thought. Surely there had to be another boy on the planet besides Scott Spencer who could make her feel like her insides were bungee jumping. But it was more than that. It was his sense of humor, and his mind, and—

Stop that, she ordered her brain. Scott Spencer is just a boy. You are not starring in a Jane Austen novel. You are starring in your own life, which from here on in is going to be—

"This must be my lucky day."

Anna turned to see a big moon face under a Funk Daddy baseball cap grinning down at her. She smiled politely. The guy, who had to be midthirties at least, stuck his briefcase into the overhead bin and then slid his Fubu'd butt into the seat next to her.

He held out a pudgy hand. "Rick Resnick. And you are . . . ?"

"Anaïs Nin," Anna said sweetly, naming a long-dead favorite writer.

"Annie, it's a pleasure."

With a nod, Anna turned back to the window. She felt a hand on her shoulder. "Tell you what, Annie, I'll get us a couple stiffies and we'll get to know each other. Miss!"

Anna was appalled. Not only was Rick Resnick culturally illiterate, he was also utterly oblivious to her lack of interest. As the DC-10 taxied to the runway, he launched into his unsolicited life story, the rags-to-riches tale of a Brooklyn boy in a garage band who'd grown up to make a mint in the music business. To accentuate a point, he'd touch Anna's hand or leg. Stuck in her window seat, Anna was as captive as she would have been tipped back at the dentist's. Since first class was completely full and Rick Resnick, whom she was starting to think of as The Seatmate from Hell, didn't come with laughing gas, she decided that vodka tonics would have to do.

Anna downed half of her second one as New Jersey passed below and Rick droned on. Maybe this was the first official test of her new life. If she could tell Rick to fuck off, which was exactly what Cyn would have done, she'd be proving to herself that things were going to be different.

Anna had a mental picture of the words *fuck off*. But they simply would not come out of her mouth. She was constitutionally incapable of saying something that rude. Okay, so this wasn't an official test, just something to get through until she could get to her new life. Anna decided to rely on the vodka; if she got sufficiently polluted, maybe she could just tune him out.

Rick Resnick touched Anna's hand again. "So dig it, I'm on the phone with Michael—this was a few years back—and his freakin' chimp starts screechin' in the background. . . ."

Anna looked around; anything was better than eye contact with Rick Resnick. Diagonally across the aisle, a guy stood to pull off his sweatshirt, revealing a V-cut hard body in a Princeton tee. At least six feet tall, with short brown hair and electric-blue eyes, he moved with the easy grace of an athlete. Between the champagne in the limo and the airborne vodka tonics, Anna was looped enough to see two of him. She closed one eye to get a better view.

Princeton Boy took it as a wink. He winked back.

Anna smiled at him—flirtatiously, she hoped, because what the hell.

"Refill?" Rick Resnick's hand was on her knee.

Anna dead-eyed his digits. "Please don't do that."

He gave her knee a little squeeze before withdrawing. "Just being friendly, Annie-bo-bannie."

Annie-bo-bannie? What a tool. She looked up again, more than ready to continue her flirtation with the guy across the aisle, but he'd sat down and picked up a book. So much for Princeton Charming to the rescue.

New drinks appeared, despite Anna's polite refusal. Rick launched into an endless story about partying with various rock stars, name-dropping shamelessly. The flight attendant offered breakfast. But Anna never ate on planes. It wasn't as if the hot towels and comfy seats somehow made the food edible. She had just managed to zone out when she felt Rick's hand squeeze hers. "Annie-bo-bannie, you are one terrific listener."

As she jerked her hand away, she caught a tight-end view of Princeton Boy on his way to the bathroom. Doubtless he'd seen her hand under Rick's. Great. She threw back the last of her third drink.

Rick was impressed. "Whoa. Who knew you were such a party girl?"

"Paige?"

Anna looked up. Princeton Boy smiled expectantly down at her. Which was like a dream come true. For some girl named Paige.

"Sorry, my name isn't—"

"I'm Jack," said Princeton Boy. "We met at . . . Oh, come on. You must remember. *Paige.*"

"Bro', her name is Annie," ever-helpful Rick chimed in.

Not true. But it wasn't Paige, either. Whoever that lucky bitch was.

Anna shook her head. "I'm sorry. I really do think you've mistaken me for someone else."

PB chuckled and shook his head. "I *know* it's you. It

was—what, last October? At Lambda Chi. This drunk-off-his-ass guy had you cornered, and you were too polite to tell him off."

Anna was about to deny it when the truth dawned; if it hadn't been for alcohol-induced stupidity, she would have caught on sooner. PB had never really met her before. He was concocting this story in an attempt to extricate her from "some drunk-off-his-ass guy" who had her cornered that very minute.

"Oh, right. Of course! Jack . . . Kerouac!" Anna playfully tapped her forehead, as if to say, How could I have forgotten?

She'd given him the name of a famous beatnik writer from the fifties and could tell by his broad grin that he got the joke. "That's me," PB agreed. "You look great, Paige. How's it going?"

"Yo, let's go to the videotape," RR interjected. "She told me her name was Annie."

Anna's eyes stayed on PB. "Actually, I told you that my name was Anaïs Nin."

"Anaïs. I like it," PB said.

RR threw up his hands. "What am I, monkey-in-the-freakin'-middle? Buddy, you never saw this chick before in your life. And we're in the middle of a private conversation here."

PB bent down to meet RR at eye level. "No offense, dude, but she doesn't want to have any kind of conversation with you. Now be cool and trade seats with me, and I won't have to report that Thai stick in your carry-on."

"Screw you, buddy! I don't have any—"

Anna smiled politely. "Then why did you offer me some—how did you put it?—'primo shit,'" she said, hardly believing her own audacity. Yes! Score for Anna!

PB pointed at his empty seat across the aisle. "It's got your name on it." RR cursed under his breath but moved. PB slid in next to Anna. A dimple played in his left cheek. "I have a confession to make. I'm not really Jack Kerouac."

"That's okay. I'm not really Anaïs Nin—not that my former seatmate would know the difference," Anna said, gesturing toward RR, who was stumbling to his new seat. "I guess he's not up on erotic French surrealism."

PB was duly impressed. "But you are. You don't look like that kind of girl."

"What kind of girl do I look like?"

He considered for a moment. "Prep-school-cool enough to drive with your legs crossed."

"That'll teach you to judge a book by its cover, Jack."

"Ben, actually." He held out his hand. "Birnbaum."

She took it. "Anna Percy." He had great hands. She didn't let go.

That was when Anna had her epiphany: It was happening. It was really happening. Thirteen years of Cynicism had not gone for naught after all. Okay, the witty repartee was fueled by more alcohol than she'd ever consumed before in her life, but just the same . . . she was flirting with Ben Birnbaum. "It was very gallant of you to rescue me, Ben Birnbaum."

"I felt your death wish clear across the aisle. What else could I do?"

"That palpable, huh?"

Ben cocked his head at her. "I'm shaking the hand of a beautiful, mysterious, and literate girl who just used the word *palpable*."

"Is that unusual?"

"Very. Plus you didn't say 'like' in the middle of your, like, sentence."

"And that's, like, unusual, too?"

"Oh yeah. Beauty and brains. Hot as hell."

At that moment, for the first time in her life, Anna felt hot. She liked it. A lot. "Want to hear more?"

He nodded.

She leaned closer. "Verisimilitude. Diaphanous. Transcendent."

He watched her mouth. "Who *are* you?"

"Does it matter?" She passed him her vodka tonic. He took a sip and handed it back to her.

"Yes, it does. Very much so."

Anna melted into her seat. He was a freshman at Princeton, flying home for a wedding. She told him her home was Manhattan but that she'd be in Los Angeles with her father for a while, doing a six-month internship at the Randall Prescott Literary Agency; then it was off to Yale in the autumn. The flight attendant announced some loser movie, and people began pulling down their window shades. They kept their conversation going through most of the movie, but all Anna could think of was how badly she wanted to tear his clothes off.

Ben brushed her hair off her face. "I want to be alone with you."

Suddenly he stood up and stepped into the aisle. His eyes flicked from Anna to the bathroom. In other words, Follow me.

This, Anna figured, *this* is the true official test of my new life.

She followed him.

The door shut behind Anna, and Ben lifted her onto the sink. They kissed until Anna couldn't breathe and then, just as Anna was beginning to truly forget herself . . .

Knock-knock-knock. Followed by a really loud, really pissed-off voice.

"THIS IS THE FLIGHT ATTENDANT. IT IS AGAINST FEDERAL REGULATIONS FOR THE LAVATORY TO BE OCCUPIED BY MORE THAN ONE PERSON AT A TIME. OPEN THIS DOOR IMMEDIATELY!"

Anna jumped off the sink, smoothing her hair and straightening her clothes. Before she could reach for the interior handle, the flight attendant had popped open the door with some supersecret device. With turquoise eye shadow and helmet hair, she looked exactly like Miss Corrigan, Anna's hated third-grade teacher.

Just as Anna and Ben stepped out into the aisle, the movie ended. Miss Corrigan gave them a quick once-over punctuated by a brisk about-face. Her silence underscored her contempt. Everyone in first class was staring at them. Rick, grinning smugly, stood with two flight attendants and one livid copilot.

The copilot shook Rick's hand. "Thank you for reporting this, sir." He turned to Ben and Anna. "Back in your seats. Now."

Anna wished a hole would open in the floor of the plane so that she could fall through and float away. No such luck. Her face burned as they sat down again. She could barely make eye contact with Ben.

"Hey, don't worry about it," Ben said as he gently took her chin in his hand and pulled her head toward him. "Look at it this way. We added dollar value to a cross-country flight. I'm sure we were more entertaining than that dog of a movie."

"I'd rather not be their entertainment. God. Maybe I can hire a hypnotist to erase it from my memory."

Ben chuckled. "You, Anna Percy, are unlike any girl I have ever known."

Since the moment they'd met, she'd been unlike any girl she'd ever known herself to be, either. But he had no way of knowing that.

Ben gazed into her eyes. "I don't want to say good-bye to you when we land."

Neither do I . . .

"I'll give you my cell number," Anna offered, in as breezy a tone as she could muster. She jotted it down on a cocktail napkin that had somehow found its way into her purse.

"I just got a crazy idea," Ben said as he stuck the napkin in his pocket. "Why don't you come with me to the wedding?"

Anna laughed. "You can't be serious."

"C'mon. It's Jackson Sharpe's wedding. It'll be a blast."

"No one invites someone they just met to a—" Anna stopped and hit mental rewind. "Wait. Did you just say Jackson Sharpe? The movie star Jackson Sharpe? He's one of the few actors I actually respect."

"I'll tell him you said so. Or you could come along and tell him yourself."

In Anna Percy's seventeen years and eight months on the planet, she'd done things that most girls could only dream of. Chatted with royalty at Wimbledon. Sat next to Christina Onassis at a fund-raiser for the Whitney. Met with the president's daughter at a symposium on high school students and geopolitics. But it all paled in comparison to the prospect of attending Jackson Sharpe's wedding on the arm of Ben Birnbaum, as the new Anna Percy.

So she said yes.

Two

"Are you sure I can't give you a ride?" Ben asked again as he retrieved the last of Anna's Louis Vuitton signature bags from the luggage carousel. "I was just going to catch a cab."

"My father said he'd meet me—I'm sure he'll be here any minute." Anna was feeling somewhat self-conscious. She'd downed two cups of black coffee before they'd landed. Now, back on terra firma and in the vicinity of sober, what had happened on the plane with Ben seemed even more like an out-of-body experience. Except that the thought of it gave her a very in-body instant replay.

He hoisted his Lambertson Truex leather duffel bag over his shoulder. "Well, I'm not heading out until I'm sure he actually—"

"Excuse me, Miss Percy?"

Anna turned to see a tall, loose-limbed young man with platinum hair and an inch of dark roots, dressed in a bad black suit and wrinkled white shirt. He had silver rings on almost every finger, including his left thumb.

20

"Yes, I'm Anna."

"Hey. I'm Django Simms, your dad's assistant," he said in a honeyed southern drawl, holding out his large hand for a firm handshake. "Call me Django. Your father showed me your photo; that's how I recognized you. Sorry I'm late. Traffic on the 405 was a bitch and a half."

"No problem," Anna assured him. She quickly introduced Ben.

"Your dad didn't mention you were comin' with your boyfriend," Django declared as he flagged down a porter for Anna's bags.

"Oh no, Ben's not—I mean . . . ," Anna stammered. "We just met."

"Oh. Lucky guy." Django's eyes flicked over Ben.

"Where's my father?"

"He said to tell you he was unavoidably detained, and he's real sorry."

"I see." Anna's shoulders tightened. Her father had promised he'd be at the airport. Which meant he was already up to his old habits: breaking promises as quickly as he made them.

"I'll have the porter bring your stuff out to the car; then I'll pick you up," Django said. "Work for you?"

"Fine," Anna replied. "Thanks."

"No prob." Django tipped a nonexistent hat in Ben's direction and then strode off with the porter toward the exit doors.

Ben scowled. "There's something about that guy."

Wow, was Ben jealous of Django or something?

Anna knew it was childish, but she hoped he was. "Well, Ben. This has been quite an unusual trip."

"Unforgettable. So. I'll pick you up at five o'clock?"

"I'm looking forward to it."

"Me too." He kissed her lightly on the lips, and then he and Anna took off in separate directions. Anna turned to watch him, walking poetry in a weathered leather bomber jacket.

Once she stepped outside, the intense sunshine was nearly blinding; she reached for her classic Dakota Smith sunglasses. It felt unnatural, in a way, being the last day of December. She started to perspire and realized that the temperature had to be close to eighty degrees. Up ahead Django hopped out of a BMW, waving to her. She strode over to him quickly, and he held the rear door open for her.

"Sorry to rush you, but they don't like cars to stand here for more than fifteen seconds at a time." He slid into the driver's seat and inched the car out into the thick airport traffic. "Your dad really was sorry not to meet you."

"I understand," Anna said, even though she really didn't. She hadn't seen her father in more than a year. And though she knew how busy he was with his investment firm, it still hurt her feelings that he couldn't take an hour off to meet her plane.

"So the plan is we'll drop your bags off at the house, then you're meetin' him for lunch at Heaven," Django continued. "In Beverly Hills. To celebrate your arrival."

Anna had never heard of Heaven. In the larger sense—heaven, hell, all that—she wasn't sure whether or not she believed that such a place existed. But if it did, she was certain that heaven did not exist in Beverly Hills. Well, at least they weren't having lunch at Spago (which was post-hip) or Buffalo Club in Santa Monica (recently written about in *The New York Times* as the hippest of the hip, meaning that it was on the road to being post-hip), or some trendy, overpriced sushi restaurant (she never could get used to eating bait). Frankly, Anna would have preferred a nameless sidewalk café or, better yet, a melted cheese sandwich at home with her shoes kicked off, followed by a short nap and a long bubble bath before her date with Ben.

"So, how long will your visit be?" Django asked as he pulled onto the freeway. Evidently her father had neglected to inform his assistant that she was actually going to live there.

"I'm not sure yet," Anna replied.

"I could arrange some sightseeing—"

"Oh, that's not necessary, but thank you."

"Well, if you change your mind . . ."

Anna nodded. It seemed odd to be riding alone in the backseat while a very cute guy who didn't look to be much older than she was drove alone in the front seat. Over the years, the mean age of her mother's drivers had edged somewhat north of fifty. Not that Jane Cabot Percy would ever have considered a driver with a spiked blond hairdo, no matter how old he was.

"Music?" Django asked.

"Sure, fine." She expected he'd put on something headbanging. But instead, the cool sounds of a solo jazz pianist filled the interior of the BMW. Anna leaned back in the tan leather seat. As she took in the palm trees, the cloudless sky, and the brilliant sunshine, she let the music carry her away.

"Ma'am? Miss Percy? Anna?"

Anna's bleary eyes flicked open. Django was twisted around in his seat, gently calling to her. The car had stopped. She felt totally disoriented. "What?" she croaked.

"Sorry to wake you. But we're here."

They were parked in the circular driveway of her father's house, on the corner of Elevado Avenue and North Foothill Drive. Her bags were already in front of the double white front doors.

"I guess I fell asleep," Anna said, yawning.

"Did you want to go in and freshen up before I take you to meet your dad? I was supposed to have you at Heaven ten minutes ago, though."

"I'm okay," Anna assured him, getting out and stretching.

"If you're sure . . ."

"I'll be fine. After a cup of coffee."

"Well, let me tell Mina to put your things away. That okay?"

"Mina?"

"One of the housekeepers."

"Oh, sure. Fine," Anna agreed. "Thanks."

The elegant house, built by Anna's grandparents in the 1950s, looked exactly as she remembered it from her last visit. It was massive, white stucco with red shutters, shaded by giant palm and eucalyptus trees. Crimson, pink, purple, and lavender flowers lined the path to the front door. The property was enclosed by shrubbery so tall and thick that it served the same purpose as a privacy fence.

Two years ago, Anna recalled, her grandparents had decided to retire to their golf course home in Palm Springs. So Anna's father had moved from his Wilshire Boulevard high-rise condo into the family homestead.

As Django disappeared into the house with her luggage, Anna brushed her hair and popped a Hint Mint. She was replacing her lip gloss when Django loped back toward the car. Anna got a really good look at him. He had intense eyes, chiseled cheekbones, and the insouciant gait of a guy who knew he was hot. He managed to make his cheap black chauffeur's uniform look casual and hip.

Django slid back into the driver's seat. "Ready to rock 'n' roll?"

"Hold on a sec." Anna got out of the car, opened the door on the passenger's side, and got in next to Django. "Much better."

He gave her a bemused look. "You fraternizin' with the help?"

"I just felt ridiculous sitting back there all by myself. Unless you mind—"

"Ma'am, any guy who'd mind having a beautiful girl like you sit next to him is deaf, dumb, and blind times ten." He pulled the BMW out of the driveway.

"You have to stop calling me ma'am," Anna insisted. "It makes me want to look around for my mother."

"Sorry. Where I come from, women like it."

"Where is that?"

"Boonietown, Mississippi—you might have heard of it?"

It took Anna a beat before she burst out laughing. Then Django laughed, too. "Seriously. Where?"

"That was long ago and far away," Django said. A blonde in a red Viper convertible behind them honked impatiently with her free hand—the one not grasping her cell phone—then zoomed around them. He shook his head. "Everyone in this town wants everything to happen yesterday."

As he powered down Santa Monica Boulevard, he popped the CD out of the CD player and handed it to Anna. "A gift. My demo."

Anna was astonished. "That was *you* on the piano?"

"Yeah."

"It was wonderful. Did you come out here to try and get signed to a record contract?"

"You think I'm like everyone else here?" Django quipped. "Chasin' some fool dream?"

Anna shook her head. "I don't understand why someone who can play the piano like that would be my father's assistant."

Django didn't offer to explain, so Anna dropped it.

Ten minutes later he pulled the car up outside of
Heaven, a restaurant supposedly so hip it bore no sign.
You just had to *know*. A valet opened the passenger
door for Anna. "Want me to wait?" Django called.

"No, that's fine."

"Well, have fun, then. Try to, anyway. Oh, hold up a
sec." Django pulled a small business card from his
pocket and handed it to Anna. "In case you ever need
me. For a ride. Or anything."

His "anything" had an interesting spin to it. In the
past she would have dismissed him as "the driver," no
matter how cute he was. That, Anna decided, was an
attitude that definitely needed adjusting.

She gave him what she hoped was a dazzling smile.
"Thanks. And thanks for the CD, too." Then she slipped
his card into her wallet and headed into the restaurant.

Three

The first thing Anna noted about Heaven was that, appropriately enough, everything was white. The walls. The suede banquettes. The curtains that separated the we're-so-famous-we-don't-want-you-to-bother-us tables from the others. It wasn't lost on Anna that the curtains were actually transparent, so the we're-so-famous could pretend they didn't want to be stared at while at the same time allowing the world to ogle.

And that, Anna thought, was just so L.A.

She sat solo at a table for two, awaiting her father. Thirty minutes and two cups of black coffee later, she was still solo. She began making a mental list of reasons her father might be unavoidably detained. But she knew her father had her cell number. Why hadn't he called?

"Miss, would you like to order while you're waiting for your companion?"

Anna blinked at the gorgeous white sari–clad waitress, who stood by expectantly with a white pencil and white pad. What the hell. She couldn't very well live on bile. She inquired as to the possibility of a grilled cheese sandwich. When the waitress blanched, she changed her order to a grilled mahi sandwich and decided that if her father didn't arrive by the time her sandwich did, she'd ask the maitre d' to call her a taxi.

She checked her watch again. Forty minutes. All around her people with the sheen of "I'm too cool to eat behind the curtains" were chattering away. She was the only person dining alone. She wondered if she looked confident and mysterious. Doubtful. She probably looked like what she was: a girl who'd been stood up.

"Your lunch." The waitress set down her sandwich, which was adorned with white bean sprouts and a single slice of organic tomato. "Can I get you anything else?"

Anna stared at her sandwich and couldn't bear the thought of eating it alone. Instead she asked for the check as the waitress frowned at the untouched lunch. Was it not to her liking? Anna had to assure her three times that she was fine, the food was fine, and, in fact, life in general was just fine, fine, fine. Evidently in Los Angeles people expected you to be as serene and sunny as the weather. In New York you could wallow in existential angst whenever you felt like it, and constant cheerfulness would only make people suspect that you were brain damaged.

Anna asked the waitress to wrap her lunch to go— perhaps her father would want dead fish. That was, if she ever found her father. The waitress whisked Anna's platinum AmEx card away and returned with the check for her signature. At that moment Anna looked through the floor-to-ceiling window and saw a disheveled older man in a baseball cap—obviously homeless—shuffling down the street. Impulsively, she grabbed her untouched lunch and rushed out onto Wilshire Boulevard, looking for the homeless man. She didn't see him, just ultrathin women and gym-obsessed men, all walking like they had someplace crucial to be.

"Hey! You look like a beautiful woman who needs a ride."

Anna's father's car was curbside, Django leaning out the passenger window, grinning behind his aviator-style Ray-Bans.

"How did you get here?"

"Came back to wait on you. You lookin' for the bum?"

Suddenly Anna felt ridiculous. "I wanted to give him my lunch."

Django cocked his head to the east. "He just walked into the Barnes and Noble on the corner. In this town you can't tell the bums from the writers."

Anna climbed into the front seat and put the sandwich on the dashboard as Django started the car. "My father never showed up."

"I know. He sent me to fetch you."

An ache clenched Anna's throat. Her father kept sending people for her but somehow couldn't manage to show up himself.

"He's home," Django went on.

"And very busy," Anna filled in, her voice tight again.

Django scratched his chin. "Uh . . . I'm supposed to

tell you somethin' about an investor's call from Hawaii
he had to take."

Anna swallowed hard. One of the reasons that her
mother always gave for the end of her marriage was that
her father was "too driven." And here he was, proving it
true once again. Well, this disappointment was between
her and her father. She'd grown up with the credo that
family laundry did not get aired in public . . . and certainly not with the chauffeur.

A few minutes later Django dropped her off with a cocky
grin and a casual salute. "Take it easy, Anna." He made that
little hat-tipping gesture again before he drove off.

Anna rang repeatedly before a shapely young housekeeper with hair a shade of red not found in nature
came to the door. She couldn't have been a day over
twenty-one. "Hello, I'm—"

"I know who you are." The housekeeper let Anna into
the cool stone foyer. When she pivoted off, Anna noticed
that she was wearing high heels with her short uniform.

"Excuse me," Anna called after her. "Do you have a
name?"

"Inga," the girl said sullenly.

"Thank you, Inga. Do you know where my father is?"

The young woman shrugged. "I saw him a little
while ago. Now, I don't know. Maybe he went out."

Anna tried to hide her irritation, which was mixed
with hurt. "How about my room? Do you know where
that is?"

"Upstairs. Last one on the right. Mina put your stuff

away." She pointed up the circular staircase at the end of the hall and then turned away.

"Thank her for me. Look, do you happen to know if my father—"

Inga returned to whatever she was doing, and Anna found herself talking to Inga's disappearing backside. She checked the entire ground floor for her dad but only encountered a cook and yet another housekeeper in the kitchen, smoking cigarettes and watching a Spanish *telenovella*. Neither paid her any attention, so she went upstairs and checked all seven bedrooms. Nothing. Great. Just great.

Anna wandered back to her own room. A handmade silk quilt in shades of pink lay across the oak canopy bed. The hardwood floor gleamed beneath tapestry rugs with hand-knotted edges. Anna found her clothes unpacked in an antique armoire scented with a lavender sachet, her sweaters and underwear folded in the dresser drawers. Each drawer had been scattered with rose petals. There were fresh flowers in a crystal vase on a small table by the picture window and an antique chaise longue. It was really everything a girl could want. That is, if what a girl really wanted was anything other than her father.

Just as Anna was about to kick off her shoes and curl up for a quick nap, there was a perfunctory knock on the door, which opened immediately. Inga stuck her head into Anna's room.

"Try the gazebo." Then the door slammed shut.

The gazebo. Her grandparents' house had been built

on something that was a rarity in Beverly Hills: a sizable plot of land. There were two acres of landscaped grounds, with a guest house, an artificial stream and small foot-bridge, a swimming pool, and a lighted paddle-tennis court. In the middle of these grounds, directly under a huge eucalyptus tree, was a New England–style gazebo large enough to seat twenty people.

Anna trudged out the back door and followed the flagstone path that led to the gazebo. The first thing she saw, standing proudly on the floor, was a five-foot-high sculpture of Cupid. His quiver was full, and he held an arrow drawn back, ready to be shot.

The second thing she saw was her father, sprawled on the wooden slats at Cupid's feet. She gasped, afraid for an instant that he was dead. Or, at the least, very sick.

Then she heard him snore. Loudly. Was he *drunk?* To the best of her knowledge, Susan was the only one in the family with an alcohol problem. There was a strange odor she couldn't place. No, wait—it was kind of sweet and skunky, and it made her feel a little light-headed—of course she could place it. Marijuana. Now she noticed the partially smoked joint inches from his outstretched right hand. Judging from how little had been consumed, it would appear her father had gained access to what Rick Resnick, that loser from the plane, would certainly term "primo shit." Not that Anna actually knew what "primo shit" was. Other than alco-hol, she'd never ingested a mood-altering substance in her life.

For several long moments Anna just stood there. Her father was a man who had his suits custom-made in London, and she knew he had a taste for Armagnac, but only as a drink to nurse after dinner. If someone had told her that she'd find her father passed out on the floor with a blunt, she'd have laughed.

Yet there it was. There *he* was. He was in his early forties, tall and lean. Though his eyes were closed at the moment, Anna knew them to be a startling blue against his perpetually tanned face. He had a new, spiky haircut and a day's worth of stubble on his cheeks. Even in his disheveled state, he looked easily ten years younger than he was. Anna shook her father's shoulder hard. "Dad. Dad!"

He snorted awake and sat bolt upright, blinking until he could focus on his daughter. "Anna?"

"Right on the first guess."

"Hey . . ." He leaned against Cupid, rubbing his face. "What time is it?"

Unbelievable. Anna glared at him. "Past the time you said you'd meet my plane. And past the time you said you'd meet me for lunch."

"Oh, man." He ran a hand over his face. "I messed up. I'm so sorry, honey." He stood up and hugged her. She barely hugged him back.

"Uh-oh. You're mad. Cut me some slack, okay? I've been getting these bitchin' headaches and the only thing that helps is weed. I guess it knocked me out."

Anna's anger instantly morphed into concern. "Have you seen a doctor?"

"Doctors." He made a dismissive gesture with his hand and sat on the filigreed iron bench, patting the space next to him so that Anna would sit, too. "I've got a killer herbalist in Topanga Canyon. So, how are you?"

"Fine." It was the automatic answer she always gave him.

"You look great. How's your sister?"

"She's back in rehab. I told you on the phone," she reminded him. Fear clutched Anna's stomach. He was acting so bizarrely. She knew her father to be an organized, PalmPilot man whose idea of casual was a three-ply cashmere sweater. But here he was, in jeans and a grungy T-shirt, using profanity. What if he really was sick? What if he had a brain tumor or some kind of weird, early-onset Alzheimer's?

"If you're getting bad headaches, you really should see a doctor, Dad."

"Hey, don't you think it's about time you started calling me Jonathan?"

"Why?" Anna asked, trying to mask how totally freaked she was by her father's transformation.

"You're all grown up, that's why. I always wanted to call my parents by their first names, but it wigged 'em out. Hey, that really sucks about Susan."

That really sucks about Susan?" Don't get too worked up over it, Dad—it was only a near overdose—not like she died or anything.

"Fine. Jonathan," Anna snapped.

Her father stood and stretched. "Let's get Teresa to

rustle us up some lunch, huh?" he suggested. "She's a monster cook."

Anna agreed. And while part of her wanted to run away and pretend this encounter had never occurred, the other part of her still hadn't eaten all day and was starving. And maybe everything her father had said was the truth. She'd read how marijuana helped ease the symptoms of some illnesses, so why not give her father the benefit of the doubt?

As they strolled back toward the house, her father asked all about Anna's life: school, guys, et cetera. She gave her usual polite and obligatory answers. Then he asked about the subject that always seemed to interest him the most: his ex-wife.

"She's how she always is," Anna tried to remind him as they went in the back door.

"Still the Ice Maid of the Upper East Side?"

"At the moment she's in Venice, thawing out."

Her father's face lit up. "No shit? She decided to come here with you?"

It took a beat for Anna to realize that her father was thinking of the Los Angeles neighborhood of Venice, south of Santa Monica, by the ocean. "Venice, *Italy*," Anna explained.

"Right. Shoulda known. Your mother wouldn't be caught· dead in Venice. Way too funky for her." He sounded disappointed. They went into the kitchen; her father asked the older woman to fix them some food. She rose wordlessly, her eyes still glued to her soap opera.

A few moments later they were in the formal dining room, eating blue corn tortilla chips and homemade tomato-and-cilantro salsa and avocado-and-chicken-breast sandwiches. Anna told her father about that evening's date with Ben, omitting the story of how she'd met him. Then she wiped her mouth and set the perfectly ironed linen napkin next to her plate. "That was delicious. I think I'll take a nap before I get ready. What are you doing to ring in the New Year, Dad?"

He wagged a finger at her. "*Jonathan*. I'm low-keying it this year. Hanging out with a friend, that's all."

Anna went upstairs and gazed out her window, which faced the backyard. She hadn't been there for more than about five seconds when she saw her father head back toward the gazebo. And then she remembered: He'd left behind that fatty he'd been smoking.

Four

Seventeen-year-old Samantha Sharpe, daughter of America's favorite movie star, Jackson Sharpe, was having a really bad day. She was in her bedroom suite (approximately the same size as a small ranch house in, say, Van Nuys), on the second floor of her father's palatial Bel Air estate (a mile, several thousand square feet, and a couple of zeros north of Jonathan Percy's mansion). She wore a silk robe over a black strapless bra and boy-cut lace panties. At the moment, most of the suite's twelve hundred square feet were covered in cocktail dress couture.

In exactly six hours and twenty-seven minutes, her father would be marrying a pregnant ingénue bimbo named Poppy Sinclair. Everyone who was anyone would be there. Photos of the nuptial extravaganza would run in every media market around the world. And Sam Sharpe still didn't have a thing to wear.

To the reception, that is.

For the ceremony she'd be poured into a hideous gold silk charmeuse bridesmaid's gown designed by

Donatella as a "personal favor" to Poppy and Jackson. As soon as the ceremony was over, Sam planned to change into something stunning. And, hopefully, *flattering*.

She'd chosen her après-ceremony dress weeks ago— a wicked Stella McCartney number in powder-blue velvet. But when she'd tried it on last night, she'd realized that it made her look like a fat pig. Why hadn't any of the so-called friends who'd shopped with her said anything? She'd end up a laughingstock in *People,* for chrissake. No, worse—she'd be the "What Was She Thinking?" fashion victim of the week in *Star*.

Well, that was *not* going to happen. Even though the photos would undoubtedly last longer than the actual marriage. She was not going to be caught for posterity looking like Kelly Osbourne in one of those god-awful velvet paintings they sold on the beach. What good were money and power if you didn't put them to good use?

So, the evening before, she'd called Fleur Abra, the wedding planner, and asked if she would be so kind as to call the design houses and have them send over some alternative dresses for the wedding reception. And presto—just like that—Sam's bedroom had been transformed into a multidesigner trunk show. Size eight, she told Fleur. Nothing conservative, and nothing in the earth colors that made her brown hair/brown eyes/ yellow-undertone skin look jaundiced.

On a rolling costume rack in the middle of Sam's airplane hangar–size closet hung the dresses Sam had eliminated: a black Chanel that made her look like she was going to a funeral, a Tom Ford in oyster pink with flounces on the hips. The *hips*. It added ten pounds. The man had to be a misogynist to design something like that. Then there was the Badgley Mischka aubergine concoction that made her look like an unpicked garden vegetable and two monstrosities by Versace that were . . . well, too Versace.

She held up a deconstructed pinstripe mess from Anne Valérie Hash to the mirror and checked out the reflection. It looked like it should be titled "When Business Suits Go Bad." Who had decided Anne Valérie was the new *It* designer, anyway?

Those were just the dresses that fit. In the couldn't-zip-it-up-if-her-life-depended-on-it pile were two Marc Jacobses, a Galliano, an Oscar de la Renta, a red Alexander McQueen, a lace Dior, and a drop-waisted Prada.

Behind her, atop her bed, were the potential accessories for the evening: a dozen assorted purses (all so tiny that she couldn't fit inside more than a lip gloss, her Valium prescription, and a condom; fortunately, that was all she ever needed to carry in an evening purse). There was also an array of jewelry from Harry Winston. The jewelry was hers; her father took her there to shop twice a year, on her birthday and Christmas. (Actually, his assistant took her.) And at the foot of the bed were towering heels by Manolo Blahnik, Jimmy Choo, and Pierre Hardy, lined up like gay soldiers on parade.

Since the items had come from several stores, each had sent a designer's assistant to help Sam with the selection process. At the moment these assistants were hovering around Sam like feeding hummingbirds, hoping that one of the girl's pudgy fingers would extend toward their dress, shoes, and/or bag, followed by the magic words "That one is perfect."

And why not? One photo in a major magazine of Sam Sharpe wearing their fashion could translate into hundreds of thousands of dollars in sales.

Sam scanned the dresses, the purses, and the shoes. The hummingbirds froze, holding their collective birdy breath.

"Thanks for the effort," Sam said. "But none of this works."

The hummingbirds exhaled their disappointment. Veronique, the Parisian assistant from Chanel, was the first to speak up. "I sink zere are sum very lovely sings."

"Zere are," Sam agreed. She padded over to the costume rack and lifted the gossamer Galliano. "However, only an anorexic could fit her thighs into this."

"Perhaps eef we try a largeer size—"

"Please, please, just take it all away." Sam plopped down on her bed, carelessly wrinkling a pale blue silk Imitation of Christ under her left thigh. Sam simply refused to wear a larger size. Approaching double digits in a dress size was worse than chronic halitosis. God, these assistants were just so passive-aggressive!

"Excuse me," the Imitation of Christ aide said, gently edging the silk dress from beneath Sam's behind. "I can return to the store and bring over three or four more, if you'd like."

"No, but thanks anyway." Sam closed her eyes. No one knew. No one understood. They thought it was all about her father's wedding to that twit, but it was more than that. Today was the most important day of Sam's seventeen years on the planet. Ben Birnbaum, the unrequited love of her life, was coming home from Princeton. He was coming to the wedding. And he was coming without a date.

She'd demanded that Fleur Abra call her the moment Ben's RSVP card arrived to be certain that he'd checked off "party of one." The call had come three weeks ago. Ben was indeed flying solo. In other words, today was her best—and possibly last—chance to bag him.

Sam had been crushing on Ben ever since that fateful day five and a half years ago when he'd French-kissed her at his family's annual Fourth of July barbecue. Maybe he'd done it because it had turned out that they were both reading—and hating—*Atlas Shrugged*. Maybe he'd done it just because he could see the sun, the moon, and the stars of his own reflection in her love-besotted eyes. Whatever the reason, it had been a defining moment in Sam's life.

Since then, she and Ben had stayed friends. He'd been a year ahead of her in school, but they'd hung out with the same people. Though she kept hoping, he'd never shown any interest in picking up where his tongue had left off, almost as if it had never happened.

It had nearly killed Sam last year when Ben had started dating one of her best friends, Cammie Sheppard. Everyone knew Cammie was a stone-cold bitch with a heart the size of a blackhead. Even after all these years, Sam was still sometimes shocked at the things Cammie would say and do in pursuit of what she wanted. On the other hand, if Cammie was on your side, your enemies were toast.

But Cammie and Ben? It just didn't make any sense to Sam. The thing about Ben Birnbaum that made him different—other than possibly the cutest ass of any guy in the Pacific time zone—was that Ben wasn't just smart: He was deep. Which was exactly how Sam saw herself. Cammie was smart, and she had an amazing talent for ruthless strategy in pursuit of whatever it was she wanted. She was also incredibly fun to hang with; Cammie equaled party equaled massive guy attention. However, in Sam's opinion, Cammie had the depth of the cup size she'd worn before she had her breasts done. So what could Ben possibly see in Cammie, except the obvious: that Cammie was gorgeous? How could gorgeous be everything to a guy as evolved as Ben Birnbaum?

The tragedy of Sam's life (other than that her mother was missing in action—she'd taken off for an ashram to "find herself" and, except for the occasional postcard to Sam sans return address, never looked back—and that her father more or less ignored her) was that no matter how hard she tried, she was still several standard deviations from gorgeous.

It wasn't like she didn't make a supreme effort. She remembered only too well a traumatic incident that had occurred when she was six years old. There had been a fund-raiser at the Chinatown Center for some cause du jour. While the parents of the Hollywood movers and shakers ate dim sum, the nannies took the children for rides on the elaborate carousel. The flaxen-haired and pouty-lipped daughters of other showbiz titans had all claimed the cool sherbet-toned animals, while she and the obese offspring of a fifty-year-old character actress had been left with the uncool dung-colored ones. It might seem trivial, pretty colors versus poopy ones, but it was all about power. After that, Sam, no dummy, had understood that extra effort was called for. For a while she'd tried passing out twenty-dollar bills to all the kids whom she'd wanted to befriend, but that had only earned her disdain as a pathetic suck-up.

By age ten Sam had turned into a chubby, hairy loner with an overbite. She had already decided to follow in the footsteps of other chubby, hairy loners and become a movie director. Growing up as her father's daughter, in the rarified world of the Hollywood A-list, she tended to see her life as a movie anyway, mentally scoring her most dramatic moments, mentally framing her most visual moments, mentally scripting her most important conversations. She'd started prowling around with a video camera, and thus, in the pursuit of cooldom, she'd ended up discovering her muse.

It was during one of these prowls that she'd come

upon her father and the live-in nanny, Aquarius, on the custom-made rocking horse that Sam's father had given her for her sixth birthday. Aquarius was doing bareback tricks on the horse, and Sam's father was riding Aquarius.

Aquarius got fired, Sam's parents got divorced, and the rest was history.

Within a year her father had remarried, to a semi-famous actress with whom he had just finished shooting a movie. A week after that, when Jackson Sharpe had gone on location to shoot a new picture, the famous actress had performed her first stepmotherly act: She'd taken young Sam to get her eyebrows, legs, and back waxed. That outing was quickly followed by others: to Dr. Attberg for invisible braces, to Fekkai's for chemical hair relaxing, and to a bariatric doctor who put Sam on a diet complete with cute little pink pills ("This will be our little secret, honey," she'd said) that made Sam run around in circles in the backyard like a terrier chasing her own tail.

When her father had returned home at the end of the shoot to find his much cuter, much thinner daughter, he'd never asked how she'd lost so much weight so quickly. But he had rewarded her by buying her a pony—a real one this time. Sam had never ridden a horse in her life, nor had she ever expressed any interest in horses. (Four years of psychotherapy later, Sam had an epiphany about the equestrian gift and the time she'd found her father and Aquarius playing Ride 'Em, Cowboy!)

Sam returned to school and discovered that now that

she was semicute, she was considered semicool. So she undertook phase two of her remodeling campaign. She started workouts at Crunch. She had her too-wide nose and receding chin done. Freshman year, she got hair extensions from Raymond and began twice weekly blowouts at Mimi's. She wore the hippest, most expensive clothes, the best makeup, and Clé de Peau Beauté's four-hundred-and-fifty-dollar-a-jar face cream. And she'd successfully moved up the social ladder.

But, dammit, she was still *not beautiful*.

As Sam got older, she figured this out: The more famous her father got, the more clout she had. Now, after two Academy Award nominations and one actual Oscar, Jackson Sharpe was very, very famous. So, though the best that could be said for Sam was that she was "attractive," she had the power of the beautiful. It wasn't nearly as good as actually *being* beautiful, but it was better than nothing.

Once Sam was in with the in-est of the in, her skills with a video camera—and access to top-notch production gear—gave her even more clout. Two-thirds of the kids at her school were wannabes of one sort or another; they all wanted to be in Sam's short films. She took a perverse pleasure in casting really gorgeous girls and making them do humiliating things on camera, like picking their nose or squeezing zits. Sam always told them it was integral to her film, which was total bullshit. What amazed Sam was that they all did whatever she told them to do.

All of this didn't make Sam as cool as, say, the daughter of a certain world-famous director who, though barely older than Sam, had already directed a big-time movie and posed for perfume ads, even though she had beady little eyes and a nose that begged for rhinoplasty. Why she didn't ax that beak was something Sam could not fathom. If Sam could've fixed her fire-hydrant calves and fat ankles with plastic surgery, she'd have done it long ago.

Sam sighed and sagged onto the bed. Even seven months preggers, her stepmother-to-be still had perfect, slender gams. So did all the girls in the wedding party, except for Sam. They'd all look just fine in those horror-show gold bridesmaid's dresses. But Sam might as well just wear a sign around her neck that screamed, "YO, BEN, CHECK OUT MY FAT LEGS!"

Well, there was no way around it. All the more reason she had to find a drop-dead, *flattering* confection to wear afterward. She had the movie moment all planned out— very *Bridget Jones.* She and Ben would dance, they'd exchange witty banter, perhaps go for a walk. They'd once had a long conversation about Machiavelli at a party where everyone else was playing Wasted Twister in their underwear. Ben would understand her pain over her father's latest nihilistic nuptials. He'd look at her with new eyes (hopefully from the waist up). He'd want to comfort her. They'd kiss, the music would swell; cut to them having mind-blowing sex, dissolve to a soft-focus shot of the two of them walking in a dewy morning rain, with Ben madly in love with her. Not with Cammie Sheppard. Nor any of her other really great-looking friends, may they all rot in hell in their size-zero Earl jeans.

"Samantha?"

Sam opened her eyes. The hummingbird designer assistants were still flitting about.

"There's a black Marc Jacobs I forgot to bring along. But now that I've seen you, I think it would be divine," a very small, very gay man suggested. He stroked the bottom of his very small, very gay goatee.

"Don't bother." She was sure that his "now that I see you" remark was a discreet way of saying, "Now that I see your ass is the size of New Jersey." She'd had enough humiliation for one afternoon. She'd just have to recycle something in her closet, much as she hated to do that. For one thing, some eager-beaver photo editor would find a still of her in the same outfit and publish the two pictures side by side. Plus, even if it was a kick-ass dress, everyone knew that the true magic of any apparel existed only the first time you wore it.

"Wow!" someone breathed from the vicinity of the bedroom door. Sam recognized the Marilyn Monroe–esque baby-soft voice without looking. It was her other best friend besides Cammie Sheppard, Delia Young.

"Hi, Dee." Sam rolled onto her stomach. Her friend, who was wearing teeny jeans and a teenier tee, carried a leather garment bag and a Louis Vuitton overnight case. They had planned to dress together for the wedding.

Dee had the flaxen hair, upturned nose, and wide blue

eyes of a porcelain doll, and a perfect little body. Whenever Sam had to have her picture taken with Dee, she always wedged half of herself behind her diminutive friend.

"Sorry I'm late—my oxygen facial took forever." Dee hung the garment bag over Sam's mirror. "So, did you pick a dress?"

"Nothing worked." So much for Sam's transformed-by-the-perfect-dress *Pretty Woman* fantasy. She turned to the assistants, who were gathered near the window. "Guys, you can go. Thanks for stopping by."

The assistants masked their disappointment and efficiently gathered up their clothes, bags, and shoes. Dee watched, a self-satisfied smile on her face, as they straggled out of the room, arms full.

"Are you smiling at my misery?" Sam asked. "Because I *so* have nothing to wear."

"Do you want to know why you love me?" Dee asked gleefully, and then hastily added, "I didn't mean that in a Georgia Sands way."

"That's *George* Sands," Sam corrected. Dee was a sweet-natured and loyal friend, but she had a bad habit of internalizing forever the personal quirks of whatever guy she dated, then leavening them with her own very average brainpower. The boyfriend before last had been a poetry major at USC who parked cars at Sunset Plaza by day and was allegedly writing the Great American Novel ("Screenplays are so ephemeral and transitory," he'd tell her) by night.

"Well, you know what I mean," Dee insisted.

"Okay, Dee. I'll bite. Why do I love you?"

"Because *I* brought you the perfect dress. Ta-da!" Dee opened the leather garment bag to reveal two dresses. One was a teensy pale pink confection that obviously belonged to teensy pale pink Dee. The other, though, immediately got Sam's interest. It was black and strapless, with a fitted black-lace-over-nude-silk bodice that gave way to a chiffon-and-net skirt that flowed to midcalf.

Sam touched the material and examined the cut. Then she slipped off her robe and pulled the dress over her head. Dee zipped her into it, and Sam regarded herself in the department-store-style mirror in the corner. It fit perfectly. The three-quarter length showed off her smooth shoulders, it was fitted where she was fit, and it hid what needed hiding. "It's genius," Sam marveled.

"I knew it!" Dee chortled. "I saw it hanging in the window at that new boutique on Rodeo next door to—"

"Who is it?"

"Donna Karan."

Sam clutched her chest. "Donna Karan? Forget it! She designs for women with fat asses."

"She does not. Besides, you're not fat, Sam. You wear a size eight."

"So? You're a zero."

Dee blew shaggy bangs out of her enormous blue eyes. "But I'm only five-one."

Sam turned her back to the mirror and peered over her shoulder to check out her fat ass. Her shrink, Dr. Fred, had told her that she had borderline body dysmorphic disorder, that she thought she saw fat where fat did not exist. Ha. She lived in Beverly Hills. Fat existed *everywhere*. All Dr. Fred had to do was to spend five minutes in the girls' locker room at Beverly Hills High and he'd see why she was the only girl who wore boy shorts instead of a thong.

But this dress pretty much hid those reasons. "What size?"

Dee looked away. "I can't recall."

Sam pulled the dress over her head, looked at the label, and gasped in horror. "This is a size *ten!*"

"So?"

"So, I can't wear a ten. What if someone found out?"

"If you don't want to wear it, don't wear it. I'll get the maid to return it. But honestly, Sam, it looks great on you."

"You think?" Sam checked out her reflection again, sucking in her stomach. It really did look good. And now she recalled that the time she and Ben had talked philosophy at that party, she'd been wearing a black cashmere tee. He'd said she looked nice, too. "Ben likes black."

"Ben?" Dee's voice was sharp. "Ben Birnbaum? What does Ben Birnbaum have to do with anything?"

Damn. Why had Sam been stupid enough to say aloud what she'd been thinking? No one knew how she felt about Ben. Like she'd ever be dumb enough to tell Dee (a girl with a pathological inability to keep her mouth shut) that she'd been crushing on him. The news would end up on a billboard above Highland Avenue the size of Hollywood billboard queen Angelyne's.

"Ben has good taste, that's all," Sam explained. "How many straight guys do you know with good taste?"

"Sam, you wouldn't have said his name unless he was on your mind or something." Dee's azure eyes widened. "Are you into him?"

"I only like him as a friend, Dee."

"Translation: I want to jump his bones," Dee quipped.

"I'm just looking out for Cammie," Sam improvised. "She wants him back."

"How do you know?"

"I was with her when she left a message on Ben's cell that she wasn't bringing a date and they should talk," Sam said patiently. "You know she still hasn't gotten over the fact that he broke up with her."

"Hmmm." Dee nibbled her lower lip. "And he *is* coming to the wedding alone."

"How do you know?"

"Cammie must have mentioned it," Dee said evasively.

"You mean he called her back and she didn't tell me?"

Dee shrugged innocently. "Maybe."

"Did he?" Sam demanded. "Not that I care, personally."

Dee looked at Sam through narrowed eyes. "Methinks thou art protesting too much."

Sam winced. Dee's last boyfriend had been a pretentious young actor from Minnesota who was forever misquoting famous works.

"It's 'the lady doth protest too much,'" Sam corrected.

Dee frowned. "Did you miss a session with Dr. Fred? Because you're very hostile."

Sam saw Dr. Fred five times a week. She was one of the few private clients he'd kept after he started his national cable television show on Lifetime. On television he had the uncanny ability to get women to share the most intimate details of their lives and then respond gratefully to whatever life-fixing advice he had to offer. Sam often wondered why it was that she needed such extensive therapy while his television clients had their problems solved in a single seven-minute segment.

"I saw him yesterday, between tapings," Sam said. "Unzip me?"

Dee did. "I mean it."

Sam pulled the dress over her head. "You'd be a bit hostile if you were about to inherit a twenty-one-year-old stepmother who couldn't pass a ninth-grade exit exam."

"Not everyone is as smart as you are, Sammie. Maybe your dad really loves her."

"Please. We both know that Daddy Dearest doesn't love anyone except himself," Sam said. "But I didn't mean to take it out on you, Dee. I adore the dress. You're a lifesaver." She leaned over, hugged her friend, and then hung the dress over the mirror.

"If you're happy," Dee breathed, "I'm happy."

Sam smiled. Dee was one of the most well-meaning people she'd ever known, and had befriended Sam long before Cammie Sheppard had deigned to acknowledge Sam's existence. Plus Dee was the kind of friend who would see a certain dress and buy it because it was perfect for you. And she'd be right. That counted for a lot.

For a brief moment she was tempted to tell Dee about her plan to bag Ben; she really needed to confide in someone. God knew she couldn't confide anything really important to Dr. Fred.

"Dee . . ."

"What?"

Sam looked down into Dee's sooty-lashed blue eyes. Dee looked so sweet. For a moment Sam felt as if she could really bare her soul. But at the last second she stopped herself. So what if Dee looked innocent and cute? Guppies were cute, too. But they still ate their babies.

"Never mind," Sam said. "Thanks again for the dress. Remind me to write you a check later." She headed into her lavish bathroom to shower, happy she'd kept her mouth shut. After all, what kind of a girl tried to bone the ex-boyfriend—Ben—of one of her best friends—Cammie—when that best friend had made it crystal clear that she wanted the boyfriend back? It would make Sam look really, really bad, which was something she really, really hated.

It was one thing to be a shit and quite another to look like one.

Five

D ee bounced up and down on Sam's bed, looking much like she had when she was eight years old. Nothing made her happier than making people happy, except maybe truly dirty gossip or fooling around in public places. The fooling around in public places thing was weird because, unlike her dear friend Cammie, she didn't think of herself as a show-offy kind of girl. Maybe it was because she was so nice (she decided that was probably it) that doing something scandalous appealed to her.

But that was just a game. Love, really, was everything to her. And what would make her happiest of all would be to be loved by Ben Birnbaum.

She stopped bouncing. It was just so odd that Sam had mentioned Ben. Maybe Sam really *did* want him. Nah. Most likely, Dee decided, Sam had been so in tune with Dee's own vibrations that she'd picked up Dee's feelings without knowing it. Dee believed in things like that.

As much as Dee wanted to confide in Sam about her

love for Ben, she didn't dare. That is, until Ben loved her back. If things worked out the way she planned, it could happen. But what if she told Sam, and—God forbid—Sam told Cammie? Dee shuddered. Being on Cammie's shit list was a fate worse than death.

Dee's opinion was that Cammie didn't deserve Ben. Last year, when the two of them had hooked up, it had nearly broken Dee's heart. Being around them was so trying that Dee would occasionally erupt in nasty hives. It was a good thing that her car-parking novelist-wannabe then-boyfriend had introduced her to high colonics. There was nothing better for ridding the body of stress toxins. And after she'd caught Car-Parking Novelist-Wannabe in his bedroom with the pool guy, she'd just marched over to Zen Nation and had all the stress toxins flushed away.

It did bother Dee that Car-Parking Novelist-Wannabe was the second guy she'd fallen for who'd turned out to be light in his driving mocs, though. She'd also had a fling with the lead guitarist of the local band Pus. He'd run off with an A&R guy from Gyro Records. Dee couldn't help wondering if she was some kind of magnet for gay boys desperate to explore the heterosexual lifestyle.

Ever since Dee's father, Graham Young, had ascended to the presidency of Gyro, Dee had met a lot of famous musicians. Forget that hackneyed What I Really Want to Do Is Direct T-shirt that everyone wore three years ago. What everyone really wanted to be was a rock star. Even Jackson Sharpe had once approached Graham Young about recording a CD, though it had never come to pass.

Ben Birnbaum was refreshingly different. His rock star dreams didn't exist. Plus he radiated "guy" guy. No DC in his AC. Dee could easily picture herself with him on side-by-side massage tables at a spa in Ojai, while two small Korean women walked on their backs. After that, he'd ravish her on a faux bearskin rug, since she didn't believe in killing animals.

She did believe, though, in inspirational visualization. It was why she'd asked their handyman to put a poster of the Big Ben clock tower on the ceiling over her bed. Next to it she'd written, *If You Can Believe It, You Can Achieve It.* It was the last thing she saw every night before she turned out the light and the first thing she saw when she woke up every morning. When her friends asked her about it, she said it was a reminder of her last visit to London.

One of the Sharpes' many servants knocked on the open door to Sam's room. *"Señorita Samantha está aquí?"*

"Shower," Dee said. "Ella washo."

"The people are downstairs for . . ." The maid gestured to her hair and face. Dee realized she meant the hair and makeup people for the wedding had arrived.

"Oh, *que bueno. Cinco minutos, gracias.*"

The moment the door closed, Dee sprang up from the bed, lifted her camisole, and gazed at her naked chest in Sam's massive mirror. Not too big, not too small, no plastic surgery needed, thank you very much. Wouldn't Ben be surprised when he saw that she'd gotten her nipples pierced? She'd had them done at the Sunset Room just the month before. It had been right after her Wednesday acupuncture appointment, and she'd gone to dance off the excess energy she had accumulated from lying still for so long. She'd had a little too much to drink that night, and before she knew it, she was incorporating flashing her breasts into her dance moves. Afterward, on the way to the bathroom, this really hot guy had stopped her and told her that he did piercings and that he was ready to do her nipples right then and there. His vibe had been so mellow that she'd agreed. He'd done an excellent job, too. Dangling from each nipple now was a tiny silver ring.

She lowered her top thoughtfully. She hoped no one would mention the incident to Ben. He might misunderstand what a liberating experience it had been for her. She'd tell him herself—say, after they'd had a meaningful hookup in one of the changing rooms at Fred Segal.

Six

After an hour's nap and a steamy shower, Anna felt much better. It didn't take long to prepare for the wedding. She'd packed the perfect dress: a simple long black satin Oscar de la Renta. And the perfect jewelry: diamond studs and a narrow white pearl necklace that had once belonged to her grandmother.

Her skin was flawless, so she never wore much makeup. A single touch of pink cream blush on her high cheekbones, a coat of understated brown mascara, a nude lip gloss, the tiniest drop of Chanel No. 5 behind her ears, and she was good to go. It ran through her mind that she should hit the Chanel counter for more than perfume. Now that she was starting a new life, there was no reason she always had to look like the Ivory Girl. She could wear red lipstick or blue eye shadow or glittery highlighter on her cheekbones if she wanted to. Who knew what smudged kohl-black eyeliner could do to change a girl's life? And while she was at it, maybe some low-slung jeans with a belly chain, and sexy little T-shirts without a bra, and—

Anna sat on the bed. The very idea of dressing like
that filled her with dread. Which is ridiculous, she told
herself. *You are here to try new things.*

Anna slipped her feet into the classic strappy
Valentino pumps she'd had forever, then brushed her
straight blond hair off her face and tied it loosely at the
nape of her neck with a narrow black velvet ribbon. Her
lip gloss, cell phone, a miniature boar's-hair brush, and
her slender wallet were secreted in her Chanel pearl
clutch. And that was that.

Ben was coming any minute, so Anna went downstairs to say good-bye to her father and wish him a
happy New Year. Once again, she couldn't find him.
She suspected he was out back at the gazebo, doing
what he'd been doing the last time she found him there.
It was very disturbing. Just so . . . not him. What had
happened to the buttoned-up, highly driven business-
man? She scribbled him a Happy New Year note and
left it on the kitchen counter.

When the doorbell rang, Anna called to the housekeeper that she'd get the door herself and opened it to
Ben in a perfect Armani tux.

His face lit up when he saw her. "Wow. You look fantastic."

"Thank you. So do you." She felt like a princess as
Ben helped her into his pearl-gray Maserati Spyder two-
seater convertible.

"I'll put the top back up; I'm sure you don't want your
hair wrecked," Ben offered as he slid behind the wheel.

She put her hand on his. "Don't worry about my hair. Leave it down."

He chuckled and started the car. "That might be an L.A. first."

As Ben pulled out of the driveway, Anna tipped her face to the afternoon sun. Everything was just so perfect—the weather, Ben, going to Jackson Sharpe's wedding. There was only one thing—Ben was with the wrong girl.

At least that was how Anna saw it. Now that she was completely sober and somewhat rested, she was appalled about how they'd met. She was nothing like the babe who'd pounded vodka tonics and jammed her tongue down his throat at thirty-seven thousand feet, her butt perched on a soap-scummy sink. There was something to be said for baby-stepping outside of one's comfort zone, but her behavior on the plane had been a pole vault. There were things she liked about that high-flying version of herself, true. But the fact that it had been fueled by alcohol gave her pause. She'd seen her sister use alcohol to blur the edges and give her courage too many times, and look where Susan had ended up.

No, Anna definitely had to tell Ben the truth. "Ben," she began.

"Anna." He grinned.

Why did he have to have such a great smile? "About the plane—"

"I know. It was amazing."

"Meeting you was amazing. It's just that—"

"Shhh. Don't spoil the moment." Ben turned up the volume

on his sound system. "Karma Police" poured from the Maserati as he headed for Sunset Boulevard. So much for true confessions. She'd tell him later. Somehow.

Traffic was magically minimal. They zoomed through Beverly Hills, West Hollywood, Hollywood, and Los Feliz and then turned north into hilly Griffith Park, leaving the city behind. Ben followed the road to the Griffith Observatory, powering past the big orange road sign announcing that the observatory was closed for renovations. Finally the storied tridomed building and planetarium came into view.

Anna was surprised. When she'd heard the wedding would be at the observatory, she'd expected massive party tents on the expansive grounds. But there weren't any. "The wedding's inside? Didn't that sign say the observatory was closed to the public?"

"Welcome to Los Angeles," Ben said. "Movie stars are not the public."

"How do you know Jackson Sharpe, anyway? You never said."

"I grew up with his daughter, Sam. She's a year younger than me."

Ben turned onto a narrow driveway strewn with rose petals. Anna found this a lovely touch, if a tad excessive. Then she realized that the tires of the car ahead of them weren't disturbing the petals because they'd been painted on the asphalt. At the end of the driveway was a valet-parking stand, where beautiful people were being helped out of beautiful cars. As Ben brought the Maserati to a gentle stop, a skinny brunette in a black Gucci sheath stepped out of a black BMW. From the driver's side came a goateed guy in a red velvet smoking jacket and trousers adorned with Elvis cartoons.

"I'm sure it's a joke, but I don't get it," Anna admitted. "Who are they?"

"Very fun—," Ben began, but stopped when he saw that she was serious. "You don't recognize them?"

Anna shook her head.

"She's one of the highest-paid actresses on TV. And he's—well, no one is quite sure what he is. Probably her latest mistake." Ben eyed her curiously. "Don't you watch television?"

"Not much. Ninety percent of it is stupid, isn't it?"

"That doesn't stop most people." He smiled at her. "But you are clearly not most people."

Now, Anna told herself. It was the perfect moment to reveal the true her: generally sober. Utterly virginal. And she would have, if a valet hadn't opened her door and offered her a helping hand. Ben flipped the valet his keys, then playfully offered Anna his arm.

"Shall we?"

The moment was gone. "We shall."

They joined a line of guests snaking up a red carpet and passed beneath a giant archway of entwined red and gold roses that spelled out JACKSON + POPPY.

"Anna Percy? Is that you?"

Anna turned and beamed as she recognized the chic older woman behind her. "Lizbette!" Anna exclaimed.

"How wonderful to see you." They air-kissed in the vicinity of each other's cheeks.

"Such a surprise, Anna. I had no idea you knew Jackson."

"She doesn't," Ben put in smoothly.

Anna touched Ben's arm. "I'm sorry, let me introduce you. Crown Princess Demetrius, may I present Ben Birnbaum. Ben, the crown princess."

"Please, call me Lizbette." The princess took Ben's hand. "Any friend of Anna's is a friend of mine—especially such a handsome one."

"The pleasure is mine," Ben said.

"Excuse me now, but I'm to meet a friend and I'm dreadfully late. Lovely to meet you, Ben. Give your mother my best, Anna dear."

Ben gave Anna a bemused look as they continued toward the building. "So. Your *friend* Crown Princess Demetrius?"

"Of Greece," Anna filled in.

"And how is it that you know Crown Princess Demetrius of Greece?"

"She and my mother were roommates years ago at boarding school. In Switzerland."

"Impressive. The only princesses I know have last names like Spelling. Or Sharpe."

"As in Sam Sharpe?" Anna guessed.

"She has her princess moments. But she can be a sweetheart, too."

Could she, now? Anna wondered if Sam Sharpe and

Ben had ever been a couple. Well, she'd just have to wait and see how they reacted to each other.

They reached a security checkpoint, where Ben had to show his invitation and ID. The invitation was scanned under an electronic reader to ensure that it hadn't been counterfeited. Then they were brusquely informed that *People* magazine had exclusive media rights and private photography was strictly prohibited.

Finally they were permitted to enter the observatory's main rotunda; it was already crowded with the rich and famous, all of who seemed to know each other. Anna had been here years ago with her grandparents and loved it. The interior looked quite different, though, having been transformed for the wedding. The massive globe was still in the center of the room, but now it was swathed in red and gold velvet. Above it a huge brass bell swung gently at the end of an iron cable. Dangling from the bell was a gold angel, shooting an arrow through a red heart.

Anna gazed up at the famed ceiling murals, the planets depicted as mythological gods and goddesses. "They must be kidding," she murmured.

"What?" Ben asked.

Anna discreetly pointed upward at naked Zeus, whose face had been replaced by a likeness of Jackson Sharpe's. Nearby, Aphrodite now had the visage of Poppy Sinclair. "I don't suppose they meant that to be ironic."

Ben slipped an arm around Anna's waist. "You have no idea how refreshing it is to be with a girl like you."

There was only so long she could put off the inevitable. "I appreciate the compliment. But the truth is, Ben, I'm not . . ." She searched for the right words.

He chuckled, charmed. "Not what?"

"It's just . . ." There was no easy way to say it. "It's like this. I drank some champagne with my friend on the way to the airport, and then I had three drinks on the plane, and the truth is, I don't usually drink much, so I was . . . well . . . trashed when you met me. And that . . . isn't really me."

"What?" Ben looked shocked.

Anna's heart sank. This was exactly what she'd been afraid of. "I'm sorry if I gave you the wrong impression. It's not like me to—"

Ben laughed and hugged her. "Anna." The way he said her name was a caress. And then, in front of movie stars and Hollywood moguls and below a forty-foot rope cable that dangled a brass wedding bell, he kissed her.

Seven

"**W**ho is *that*?" Sam yelped.

"I have no idea," Dee replied.

They stood on the balcony overlooking the rotunda, watching Ben kiss a tallish, slender blonde who, at least from a distance, appeared to look nauseatingly perfect in an entirely natural sort of way.

"He brought a date," Sam surmised, her heart sinking.

Dee sighed. "He wasn't supposed to bring a date."

Sam, clad in her Versace horror-show bridesmaid's dress, mentally compared herself to Ben's mystery wench and felt instantly inadequate. Not that she planned to let Dee in on that information.

"Poor Cammie," Sam said. "She'll freak."

Dee nodded. "Poor Cammie."

They watched the girl with Ben throw her head back and laugh. "She looks familiar, doesn't she?" Sam asked.

"Whoever she is, she's beautiful."

Sam thought, *Trust Dee to state the obvious.* The girl with Ben had the kind of effortless beauty that no amount of plastic surgery could replicate. You had to be born with it. The bitch.

Dee pursed her lips. "Maybe Ben didn't bring her. Maybe she's a friend of Poppy's and they just met."

"Dee, he's got his hand on her ass."

"That's the small of her back."

"A technicality. Obviously she's his date."

"I think she's kind of tall for him."

"Great, let's go tell him that," Sam said, sagging at the prospect of having to compete with that girl, whoever the hell she was. "God, I hate this dress. I hate this wedding. I hate my life. My father probably wouldn't even notice if I left. So what if Poppy is one bridesmaid short? She's got nine more. She's all he cares about, anyway."

"You know Dr. Fred said that you and Poppy shouldn't compete for your father's affection," Dee reminded her.

"My father and I would kind of have to see each other once in a while for that to work. Anyway, I'm such a pig."

"You are not," Dee said supportively.

"Look at Ben's date! Grace Kelly—and we're totally talking circa *Rear Window*, pre–Princess of Monaco here. She's a size four at the most. And she's like three inches taller than me."

"Kiss-kiss," a voice sang out, and Cammie Sheppard came gliding over. Her signature "I-just-got-out-of-bed" strawberry blond locks fell halfway down her back, looking stunning against her pale green Balenciaga leather corset dress. She did a three-sixty to show off the velvet ribbons that laced down to the top of her perfect, heart-shaped behind.

Sam took in Cammie's fabulousness and felt depressed all over again. Cammie had bee-stung lips and deep-set honey-colored eyes. Naturally slender, her legs went on forever. True, she'd purchased the 34C breasts and had her ordinary brown hair chemically transformed into that riot of fiery curls, but so what? The total package screamed *goddess*. "Oh my God." Cammie reeled as she took in Sam's bridesmaid dress. "You look like an Oscar in drag."

"Cammie," Dee chided, "*someone* needs to clear her chakras."

"Dee, why don't you just tattoo 'New Age loser' on your forehead," Cammie snapped, "and save us all the agony of having to hear your voice."

Dee pouted. That remark was mean even by Cammie standards. Maybe she was PMSing or something. On the other hand, she knew that meanness was in Cammie's genes. Her father was an *über*-agent at Creative Artists Agency, notorious for being a son of a bitch in a business where the title really meant something.

"I'm changing as soon as the ceremony's over," Sam told Cammie. Down below, she watched Ben take two flutes of champagne from a geisha-garbed drag-queen waiter (Poppy had gushed to Sam that He-Geisha was the caterer of the moment) and clink glasses with the mystery wench.

"Ahi roll?"

A he-geisha had appeared out of nowhere, offering a tray of sushi. "No thanks." Sam waved him off and took Cammie's hand. "Okay, don't freak, but Ben's here."

Cammie's doe eyes lit up. "Why would I freak? If he's really naughty, I might even take him back."

Dee and Sam exchanged a look, and then Dee pointed discreetly toward the main floor of the rotunda, where Ben and his mystery date were chatting up some of Ben's friends from high school.

Cammie's alabaster cheeks went blotchy. "Who the hell is that?"

Dee folded her arms. "From the point of view of the Zohar, that isn't the healthiest response you can have."

"One class at the Kabala Center doesn't make you Madonna," Cammie blazed.

"Six," Dee said, wounded.

"Whatever. I saw Ben's sister at Yoga Booty yester-day, and she *specifically* told me he was coming solo."

"Sam?"

The girls turned to find the wedding planner, Fleur Abra, tapping impatiently on her Lucite clipboard and glaring at Sam.

"What?"

"What are you doing up here?" Fleur demanded, momentarily clicking off the walkie-talkie radio headset she wore. "You're a bridesmaid. They're taking photos in the East Hall right this minute. Get down there."

"I don't really photograph well." Sam went back to

Ben-watching. The mystery girl took Ben's arm. This event was supposed to end up like *Circle of Friends*, meaning that while Sam wasn't the thinnest or the cutest, she'd end up with the guy anyway. However, at the moment, it didn't look like the mystery girl had been clued in to Sam's plot line.

Well, Sam figured, that would just give the plot more dramatic arc. She'd just have to hang in there and be sweet and wonderful and plucky and—

"Sam!" Fleur interrupted Sam's mental rally. "These are your father's *wedding* photos. You should *want* to be in them."

"I've already been in a set of my father's wedding photos, Fleur. Seven years ago. I think that's a lifetime quota."

"Don't you even care how your father feels?"

"He won't notice," Sam said, her eyes still on Ben and the beautiful girl.

"I'm sure that isn't true," Fleur said, sucking in her bony cheeks. "What is the matter with you Hollywood brats? Do you think that the whole world has to revolve around you all the time? Are you deliberately trying to ruin this day for your father and Poppy? Is that what you want?"

Before Sam could respond, Cammie moved in. "What's your name again? Fluoride?"

The wedding planner pressed her lips together in a thin, angry line. "Fleur. *You* can call me Ms. Abra."

"What she *wants*, Fluoride," Cammie continued, ticking things off her fingers, "is (*a*) for her father to still be

married to her mother and her mother to come back
from her fling with the Dalai Lama; (*b*) Heidi Klum's
legs; (*c*) world peace; and (*d*) a bridesmaid's dress that
doesn't look make her look like Bigfoot playing dress-
up. So unless you can make those things happen, I sug-
gest you get the hell out of my friend's face."

Fleur's recently reconstructed nostrils (Sam knew
cocaine damage when she saw it) quivered indignantly as
she marched off. Sam smiled gratefully at Cammie. No
one could tell someone off the way Cammie could tell
someone off.

"Thanks," Sam said.

"Don't mention it." Cammie extracted a compact
from her Prada bag and checked her pale pink Stila lip
gloss. "So, what I think," she told her reflection, "is that
we should go down there and make a grand entrance. I'm
just dying to meet Ben's little friend. Do I get backup?"

Sam and Dee agreed to flank Cammie in her hour of
need. They each popped the Kate Spade mint that had
been handed to them upon entry, tossed their hair, and, in
Sam's mind, looking not unlike the trio of hot and nasty
girls in *Jawbreaker* (the movie sucked, but the clothes had
been to die for), headed for the circular stairs that led
down to the rotunda. Time to meet, greet, and compete.

Eight

Just as Ben felt the touch of Anna's hand on his arm, a slant of afternoon sun on reddish golden tendrils across the rotunda caught his eye. There was only one girl in the world with hair like that. Cammie Sheppard. And she was heading right for him, with Sam and Dee in tow.

Ben couldn't help but notice that Cammie still moved like walking sex. She was the hottest girl he'd ever known in his life—Cammie Sheppard could make the Iceman cometh. Even when he hadn't liked her, he'd loved having sex with her, after which he hadn't liked himself very much. But he was over her now. He wasn't about to let his life be ruled by the head below his waist.

As Ben watched the approach of the unholy trinity, it occurred to him that he should have prepared Anna for this moment.

"Anna, see those three girls?" he said quickly, cocking his head toward the advancing army. "The brunette is Jackson Sharpe's daughter. The other two are her best

73

friends. They were a year behind me in high school, we all hung with the same people, and—"

Too late.

"Ben!" Dee squealed.

"Hey, Dee," Ben said easily.

She stood on tiptoe to hug his neck. Sam threw her arms around him. Cammie was confident enough to be last. She made sure that there was pelvic contact when they kissed.

Which was not lost on Anna. There was something about these girls that put up Anna's defenses. She slipped an arm through Ben's. "So, introduce me to your friends," she told him.

He did. The girls told Anna how thrilled they were to meet her. How much they loved her dress. How cute her shoes were. Anna said she'd forgotten how chilly it got at night in Los Angeles; cool enough for a jacket but obviously not for her winter coat. Cammie immediately volunteered to lead a shopping expedition to Fred Segal.

"You don't wear fur, do you, Anna?" Dee queried. "Because it's like I can still hear the animals screaming when I look at their little pelts."

"You're wearing leather shoes, Dee," Cammie pointed out. "Those are made from their little *skins*."

"Eew," Dee whined.

"So Ben," Sam began, "I thought you were coming alone to the wedding."

"I was. But I called the wedding planner from the plane

and told her assistant there'd been a change of plans. She said it was fine."

"I hope it's not too inconvenient," Anna added.

"It is *so* no problem," Sam assured her.

"Firecracker shrimp?" a he-geisha offered. There were no takers.

"I love the waitstaff," Anna commented. "It took me a minute to realize they were men."

Sam lifted a champagne flute from a passing he-geisha's tray. "Not all," she confided. "One of them is a woman. We're supposed to wonder who has what equipment under those kimonos. Like anyone cares."

"If I get bored enough, I'll do hands-on research." Cammie winked, flashing a Cheshire cat smile at Ben.

The way Cammie was looking at Ben and the way he was avoiding looking back put Anna's girl-dar on red alert. Any idiot could see that the two of them must have been an item. Cammie Sheppard was one of the most beautiful girls Anna had ever seen, luscious in a way that made Anna feel prepubescent. Plus she seemed to have Cyn's self-confidence. Cyn, though, was a sweetheart, and Anna had a strong feeling that Cammie was, well . . . not.

God. What if Cammie and Ben were Cyn and Scott all over again? But then Anna smiled. She was the one with Ben, not Cammie. This time *she'd* gotten the guy.

As the three girls continued their banter, Anna leaned gently toward Ben. He eased an arm around her waist. If her earlier confession about the girl on the plane not being the "real Anna" had fazed him, he didn't show it at all.

Anna hoped that was because he'd taken it all in stride.

"So, Anna. We're all dying to know how you and Ben met," Dee gushed.

"At Princeton," Ben said instantly. "There was a kegger at the Lambda Chi house after the Yale football game. Some drunk linebacker was hitting on her—"

"And Ben came to my rescue," Anna said, delighted to play along with the new and improved how-we-met story. It was like a secret code that only they shared. "We ditched the party, took off in his Jeep, and drove to the beach."

"Long Beach," Ben added.

"To watched the sunrise," Anna concluded.

Dee sighed. "Stuff like that never happens to me."

"Ben Birnbaum, I am truly impressed," purred Cammie. "I've always known you to be more the take-no-prisoners/do-her-against-the-wall type."

Cammie was referring to an experience she and Ben had shared one night backstage at the Viper Room. Too much Cuervo Gold could make a girl lose her inhibitions. Not, Cammie realized, that she had very many of those to begin with. Ben had been quite a different Ben back then. At least, so it seemed to Cammie.

"I guess Anna brings out a different side of me," Ben said.

"That's so sweet, Anna," Cammie oozed, then mentally added, *Die, bitch.*

"How long have you two been together?" Dee asked.

Ben cocked his head at Anna. "What is it, three months now?"

"Two and a half," Anna corrected. "But it feels like—"

"Dee, baby!" A short guy in his midthirties, clad in a black leather tuxedo jacket and black jeans, interrupted them. He held out his arms to Dee, who squealed, took a running leap, and jumped into them.

"I heard Bobby and Whitney were being psycho again. Daddy didn't think you'd make it," Dee said, hugging the man again. "I'm so glad you're here!"

Which was more than either Anna or Ben could say. Anna's jaw headed south as she watched Ben's face go as white as his French-cuffed shirt. Because Dee was in the arms of none other than Anna's seatmate from hell, Rick Resnick.

Then Rick saw Anna and Ben. A malicious grin split his face. "Well, well, well, if this isn't a friggin' movie moment. Annie-bo-bannie and the frat brat!"

Dee looked confused. "Do you guys know each other?"

Rick wagged a finger at Anna. "I met her on the plane from New York."

"Look, don't be an asshole about this," Ben muttered.

"*Me* an asshole?" Rick asked. He turned to Dee. "That's when the frat brat met her, too."

"Wrong," Sam said. "They go to Princeton together."

"My lily-white ass they do," Rick hooted. "I'm telling you, they met on my plane. She was sloshed and looking for a good time, he made a move; next thing I know, badda-bing, badda-bam, they're going at it in the first-class john." He pumped his fist for graphic emphasis.

Heat rose to Anna's face. "That's not what happened. We didn't . . . I didn't . . ."

Cammie's face lit up. "Oh my God, it's true."

"We don't owe them any explanations," Ben muttered to Anna.

"Ben, how *could* you?" Sam cried, milking the moment for all she was worth. She put her hand to her heart. "You brought some B-list slut to my father's wedding? God, she probably did you for the invite!"

If there was one thing Anna knew she was not, it was a "B-list slut." She also knew that anything she or Ben might say in their defense would make only make them look guiltier. She'd thought getting caught on the plane was humiliating, but it was nothing compared to this moment.

An image sprang into Anna's mind of the damn Cupid statue in her father's gazebo. Cupid was the Roman god of love. At that moment Anna wished with every fiber of her being that she was Cupid. Because Cupid could grow wings at will and simply fly away.

Nine

At the main entrance to the planetarium ushers escorted the guests to their seats along aisles strewn with rose petals—real ones this time. The seats had all been reupholstered for the occasion in gold silk hand-painted with curlicues of red roses.

Cammie Sheppard took all this in with little reaction. She sat with her parents in the tenth row, scratching a French-manicured nail against one of the painted roses on her seat cushion. "If this shit comes off on my dress, I'll sue them," she told her father.

Clark Sheppard proudly patted her knee. "That's my girl."

Her stepmother, Patrice, shot Cammie an evil look. That was nothing new. Cammie knew Patrice loathed her. Which was fine with Cammie, who loathed Patrice right back.

Cammie's real mother had been an elementary school art teacher who died in a mysterious boating accident when Cammie was only eight. That night Cammie had been at Dee's house for her very first

79

sleepover. When her father had come to Dee's the next
day and broken the terrible news, Cammie hadn't
believed him. How could her mother be there one day
and gone forever the next? They'd been painting a
Charlotte's Web mural on her bedroom wall together;
surely her mom would come home to finish the project.

But the mural was never finished. Cammie would
never let anyone touch it, either. The half-completed
panorama still adorned one of her bedroom walls. She
never spent the night at anyone else's house, either. She
was embarrassed to admit it because she knew it was
irrational: She feared that if she spent a whole night
away from home, her father would die.

When Cammie's mom died, her father had been a
junior agent at William Morris. The family was living in
an area called "Beverly Hills adjacent," meaning in the
shadow of true power and wealth without actually pos-
sessing it, which galled the hell out of Cammie on a
regular basis.

Two years later her father married Patrice Koose, a
has-been actress on the William Morris roster who
longed for a comeback. Her father had finagled Patrice
the role of Natalie Portman's mother in a low-budget
indie flick about a mom who fought for her daughter
after she'd been sold as a sex slave to Russian gangsters,
which won her a Golden Globe nomination. After that,
it seemed to Cammie that every has-been in Hollywood
flocked to her father for representation. It began
with the oh-my-God-I-thought-she-was-dead has-beens,

followed by the please-she's-over-forty-for-God's-sake has-beens, followed by the thirty-year-old-on-the-verge-of has-beens. And after *that*, Creative Artists Agency, otherwise known as CAA, the most powerful talent agency in Hollywood, had wooed Cammie's father and his clients away from William Morris with an offer of a corner office. The big bucks started rolling in, and Clark Sheppard moved his little family to a mansion in the zip code of good and plenty, 90210.

Cammie had wanted to move, since compared to that of every kid she knew, her house was a piece of shit. However, she'd wanted the *Charlotte's Web* mural that still adorned her wall, the last tangible evidence that her real mother had existed, even more. So she threw an impressively operatic screaming tantrum. Her father had responded by insisting that the builders of their new home incorporate the mural into her new bedroom, and they had.

The night that Patrice told her new husband she hated children and the best she could offer was to stay out of Cammie's way, Cammie happened to be listening to their conversation through a bathroom vent. So in essence, Cammie was raised by a string of nannies. The upside to this was that she never had to study in Spanish 1, 2, 3, or 4. Cammie decided that if Patrice was going to ignore her, Cammie would do likewise. In her mind, Patrice was just that bitchy woman who lived in her house.

Cammie had kept her end of the bargain. Her step-mother, on the other hand, had taken every opportunity she could to make Cammie's life a thing of misery. Nothing was off-limits: the guys she saw, her brains, grades, clothes.

Patrice eyed Cammie's cleavage and sniffed. "A little obvious for a wedding, Cammie. You look like you're peddling it at Hollywood and Vine."

Jealous cow. Cammie made her wrist limp and quickly shook it back and forth. "What's this?"

"I have no idea," Patrice replied coldly.

"Your neck wattle. Time for a little touch-up, Patrice. But I'm sure you've got Dr. Birnbaum on speed dial."

"You're a bitch, Camilla."

"Takes one to know one."

Clark Sheppard chuckled. Typical. Cammie knew her dad liked to pretend that their sparring was all in fun. Cammie crossed her arms and turned away from her stepmother. A couple of rows in front and a little to the left, she could see Ben and Anna seated together. Ben's mom and dad, Dr. and Mrs. Dan Birnbaum, had joined them. Ben and Anna were deep in conversation, and Ben cut his eyes back toward Cammie for a moment. She gave him a slow, sultry smile.

Good, she thought. Very, very good.

The truth was that Ben Birnbaum was the first boy Cammie had really, truly, deeply fallen for. Not that she'd ever told him that. He'd never said "I love you" to Cammie, and she wasn't about to say it first. But she did love him. She'd even come close to breaking her never-wake-up-away-from-home rule for him because he made her feel so safe. She'd never let on to her so-called best friends that Ben was more than hot sex, either. Cammie wasn't about to give anyone that kind of power over her.

She snuck another look at Ben's pickup chick. Frankly, after the public humiliation that record producer asshole had just put her through, Cammie was amazed she'd stuck around for the ceremony. That could only mean that the girl had some balls and that Ben really was into her, even though they'd only just met. Shit.

"Hey, Cammie."

She turned to the friendly male voice behind her and saw Adam Flood slip into a seat his parents had been saving for him. The year before, Adam had been the new guy at school. Loose-limbed and cute in a Ben Stiller way—if Ben Stiller had been about six inches taller and habitually dyed his hair different bizarre colors—Adam was so funny and nice and nonthreatening that he'd effortlessly worked his way onto the school A-list. It didn't hurt that he quickly became point guard on the varsity basketball team, spoke Russian, and was a nationally ranked chess player. Since the last time Cammie had seen him, Adam's hair had gone from Elvis black to semiblue.

"Nice 'do," Cammie told him, smiling.

"It's awful," Mrs. Flood commented, though she had a loving look on her face when she said it. Adam had once told Cammie that his parents had met in law school at the University of Michigan. A couple that had met in law school, gotten married, had kids, and lived happily ever after? To Cammie, it seemed like some kind of fairy tale.

The Floods had moved from Ann Arbor to Beverly Hills, and Adam's parents had joined a prestigious entertainment law firm. They handled Jackson Sharpe's legal work and lived a few blocks from Cammie. Cammie figured they had to be reasonably wealthy, yet they were utterly unpretentious—almost unheard-of in Cammie's social circle. Their home was quite a bit smaller than Cammie's. Mr. Flood drove a Prius. His wife drove a Saturn. As for Adam, he didn't even have his own car, which was completely unheard-of for a teenager in Beverly Hills.

Cammie liked to spend time with the Floods; it was like studying prehistoric relics from another age, where families stayed together and actually seemed to like each other.

Adam gazed around at the planetarium. "Hey, if only I'd known, I'd have gone with a *Star Trek* thing."

Cammie laughed. "You probably would've done it, too."

Adam's mother nudged him. "Who's that blond singer who writes poetry that you like so much? I saw her right over there."

"Nice, Mom," Adam said.

"Have you ever seen so many movie stars in one place?" his dad asked.

Adam hitched a playful thumb at his parents. "They're still starstruck," he told Cammie. "So, where is everyone?" Cammie, as usual, was fully up-to-date on the matter and at the ready with a comprehensive list of names, in descending order of importance. "Well, you know where Sam is. Last time I saw Dee, she was with some zit in a suede tux. Knowing Skye and Parker, they're probably on the roof smoking the hash she brought back from Morocco. Krishna's parents paid her to come, so she's somewhere with Damian. Ashleigh and Jordan are in Vail—"

"Hey, there's Ben Birnbaum." Adam cocked his chin in Ben's direction. "Looks like he brought a date. Wow."

For Cammie, no translation was necessary. Obviously Adam had just seen the girl with Ben, and "wow" was his considered opinion of her. This was not going to do. Ben simply could not possibly be with another wow-inducing babe.

In the far reaches of the planetarium a string quartet began a classic love song. The ceremony, a bit late in starting, would begin any minute now; Cammie was sure it wouldn't be very long. People in Beverly Hills knew how fleeting an institution marriage could be, so they expected a short ceremony followed by a long, lavish party. Which meant Cammie didn't have much time to figure out how to deal with Ben's date. Something had to be done, but what?

Her only requirement: something that wouldn't necessitate jail time.

Ten

When Anna saw Poppy Sinclair float down the aisle, she gasped. Even many months pregnant, Poppy was a beautiful young woman. But her wedding gown, with its thousands of bugle beads surrounded by sequins and pearls, plus the enormous train, was so over the top that Poppy looked like Barbie interpreted by Roberto Benigni. On acid.

The entire wedding procession was like that. First, two little girls in exact miniatures of Poppy's bridal gown preceded her, tossing rose petals from gold baskets. Then ten bridesmaids in deeply awful dresses. Considering how incredibly rude Sam had been to her, Anna took some pleasure in seeing how unflattering the dress was on Sam. She looked like a semi-ugly gilded ducking amid nine golden swans. The bridesmaids were escorted by ten gold-vested groomsmen. Jackson Sharpe, who winked and mugged for his friends, followed them. And then finally Poppy, whose twenty-foot bridal train was held off the red carpet by eight young boys wearing Little Lord Fauntleroy knickers and riding jackets.

The ceremony was mercifully brief. Not that Anna could keep her mind on it. After her disastrous second encounter with the charming Rick Resnick, she'd wanted to make a graceful exit. But Ben had insisted they stay, saying that none of those people mattered. Reluctantly she'd agreed.

"I now pronounce you soul mates," said the minister, a woman she vaguely recognized from a *New York Times* article about New Age religious leaders. With those words, Jackson Sharpe embraced Poppy, the couple shared a long kiss, and the *People* photographers immortalized the moment from every conceivable angle. Then Jackson Sharpe—whose late father had been Jewish—smashed a wineglass under his heel, and the string quartet began "Endless Love."

"Quite an experience," Ben said to Anna with a chuckle as the wedding recessional began. He consulted an engraved card that had been handed to him when they'd entered the observatory, which laid out the schedule for the wedding. "It says here that we'll be having dinner out on the main lawn."

"But we came from that direction, and there weren't any tents."

"Hey, if Poppy wants it, the best party planners in the west can build it. I'd bet on it." He took Anna's hand, and they followed the crowd down another of the ubiquitous red carpets. This one stretched from the main rotunda into the night.

Once outside, Anna was amazed at the transforma-

tion. Floodlights beamed skyward, like at a movie pre-
miere. A giant circus tent had been erected, with warm-air
blowers to keep the temperature balmy. Countless round
tables and chairs circled a wooden dance floor. The walls
were decorated with floor-to-ceiling posters from
Jackson and Poppy's films, and an orchestra on a raised
stage played the love theme from *Romeo and Juliet.*

"Aren't you glad we stayed now?" Ben asked.

Mostly. At least the more stubborn part of Anna
was—the part that didn't want to let those crowing girls
win so easily.

"It is amazing," Anna allowed.

"Amazing," Ben agreed, smiling down at her. "Dance
with me."

Anna's lips tugged upward in a smile. "I think protocol is to wait for the bride and groom."

"Ah, clearly you don't know about the Hollywood
second-or-more-marriage-for-the-groom proviso."

Ben's blue eyes twinkled at her. Anna felt as if she could
fall into their endless blue. "And what would that be?"

"Protocol isn't broken unless you're actually *on* the
dance floor. Which, you'll notice, we aren't."

Right there, between tables, Ben put his arms
around her, and they began to dance. For Anna everything—the tables, the tacky decor, her lingering con-
cerns about the incredibly rude girls she'd met, her
inauspicious afternoon with her father, even obnoxious
Rick Resnick—seemed to melt away.

When the band changed songs, Anna and Ben found

their seats. To Anna's dismay, they were seated with Cammie and Dee; Sam was at one of the tables reserved for the wedding party. Except for Anna, everyone at the table knew everyone else, so Ben introduced her around. To her right was Adam Flood, a cute, blue-haired, open-faced guy who seemed like an actual human being. Besides Adam, Cammie, and Dee, there was a Parker, a Skye, a Damian, and a Krishna, who were obviously stoned out of their minds, plus others whose names Anna couldn't remember.

At each gold place setting was a small wrapped box from Tiffany. Anna opened hers. Inside was a gold charm bracelet with one heart-shaped charm mono-grammed with Jackson and Poppy's names. Ben's box held a gold money clip with the same monogram.

Krishna dangled the charm bracelet as if it were used tissue. "This is *so* tacky." Then out of nowhere she added, "So, Anna, I heard you and Ben did the nasty six miles over Denver."

Damian, who had dark hair, an indolent face, and blinding diamond studs in both ears, hoisted what looked to be a glass of scotch in Anna's direction. "My kind of girl."

Wrong, Anna thought. Horribly and totally wrong. Word had clearly gotten around, and it was all she could do to keep her mouth shut, so badly did she want to correct this misconception. But she knew how she would sound: guilty. Under the table Ben gave her hand a squeeze of solidarity.

The he-geishas had removed their makeup and changed into ordinary tuxedos to serve dinner. They set prawn-and-pear salads before each guest; the stoned kids lit into the food before everyone else at the table had even been served.

"So Anna, how did you and Ben really hook up?" Skye asked, stabbing enthusiastically at a prawn.

Cammie and Dee tittered, which helped Anna decide the best defense was a good offense. "Actually, Ben and I did meet on the plane. Other elements of the story may have gotten exaggerated. Anyway, I know quite a few people here."

"In the biblical sense?" Cammie asked, ignoring the appetizer and motioning for more champagne.

"Meow," Skye purred, laughing.

"Give it a rest, Cammie," Ben instructed.

"Touchy, touchy," Cammie said, as if the whole conversation was just too, too amusing.

"What Anna and I did or didn't do, where we met, how we met, or anything else about us is not going to be dinner conversation, so how about if we just change the subject?" Ben looked over at Parker. "How's showbiz?"

"Oh, you know," Parker said vaguely. "I'm up for a few things."

"Parker has the lead in all the school plays," Dee explained to Anna. "Did you ever hear of a movie called *Killing Spree IV?* He was the mean boyfriend who gets flattened by a runaway Segway."

"I must have missed it," Anna said politely.

"Most people did," Dee said. "It went right to DVD."

"No offense, dude, but that movie sucked muchly," Damian opined.

Parker shrugged good-naturedly. "I know. Hey, no one starts in the big time. Gotta pay your dues." He added a wink in Anna's direction.

Anna loathed guys who winked. Except for Ben, of course. When he'd winked at her on the plane, he'd raised the gesture to an art form. "God, everyone in this town thinks they're a future star," Skye groaned. "It's so totally boring and predictable."

"You're just feeling negative because your moon is in Jupiter," Dee explained as she nibbled on the tiniest bit of prawn. "I used to do charts," she added for Anna's benefit. "What sign are you, Anna?"

"Obviously not a Virgo." Damian smirked.

"Shut up," Ben said with a tight smile.

Dee turned to Cammie. "You know, you're a Scorpio and Ben's an Aquarius, which pretty much spells disaster. Maybe that was the problem. You know. The reason you guys broke up."

Cammie smiled coldly and rose. "Anyone else need the ladies' room? Dee?" she asked pointedly.

"Oh. Okay." Dee rose, too, and the two girls strode off.

Ben leaned toward Anna. "I'm sorry if this is uncomfortable for you."

"It's not a problem." She was careful to keep her face neutral and took a sip of her wine. She'd already guessed about Ben and Cammie, she reminded herself. There was no need to react.

"I was going to tell you about Cammie—"

"You don't owe me any explanations, Ben."

"So Anna," Parker began as he buttered a roll, "when do classes start again for you guys?"

It took Anna a moment to realize that he thought she went to Princeton with Ben. "I don't go to Princeton," she explained. "Actually, I'm still in high school. Or I would be, except . . . it's complicated."

Parker sipped his champagne. "No shit. I thought for sure you were already in college."

"So are you going to stay and go to school here?" Skye asked.

"Actually, I'll be doing an internship at Randall Prescott Literary Agency."

"Are you kidding? My mother is an agent there," Skye exclaimed. "Wait, you mean you get out of doing senior year?"

"I finished junior year with enough credits to graduate, actually, so—"

"No way," Skye insisted as she slathered a roll with butter. "God, I'd love to bag the rest of senior year. I am so over Beverly Hills High." She took a huge bite of the roll.

"Jeez, Skye, why don't you have a little roll with your butter?" Krishna asked, staring with distaste.

"I've got the munchies." Skye took another bite of her roll. "Besides, it's not like you couldn't lose a few l-b's."

"Hel-*lo*, who zipped up size-zero jeans at Barneys last week?"

"Screw you," Skye said. But she put the roll down.

That there was competition to be the thinnest was nothing new to Anna—so many of her friends in Manhattan had the same obsession. Anna knew how fortunate she was to be naturally slender. She'd taken ballet for years because she loved it; it was her main form of exercise.

Anna was glad when Adam began asking her questions about her move to Beverly Hills, since people kept coming over to their table to chat up Ben about Princeton. Obviously Ben had a lot of friends. Anna didn't mind that. She wouldn't even have been upset by an encounter with Ben's ex-girlfriend. That is, if Ben's ex-girlfriend had been something other than Medusa in stilettos. If only Anna could have done what Athena had done and turned Cammie's gorgeous hair into writhing snakes. Well, she couldn't, so she'd just have to put up with the girl.

One thing was for sure: Having Cammie Sheppard as an ex didn't say anything good about Ben at all.

Eleven

"I thought we were going to the ladies' room," Dee reminded Cammie, practically trotting to keep up with Cammie's long stride.

"Well, we're not." Cammie pushed out a door with a large red Exit sign above it. Fortunately, no alarms went off. The girls were behind the observatory, where there was nothing but a patch of grass that led into dense woods.

Cammie opened her purse and rummaged around until she came up with half a joint. "Light?"

Dee found some matches in her purse and handed them to Cammie.

Cammie read the cover. "Art's Delicatessen in Studio City?"

"My father eats there," Dee said defensively.

Cammie shrugged, lit the joint, and held it out to Dee.

"No thanks. There's all kind of chemicals in weed these days. I don't smoke unless I know who grew it."

Cammie took another hit. "More for me. So, what do you think of her?"

"Who her? Oh, *her,* her. Ben's her."

94

"Ben's her, my ass. They just met, Dee," Cammie reminded her friend. "So, I'm hotter, right?"

"Maybe Ben cares about more than surface appearances."

"That wasn't the question."

"Well, she's classic, in a certain way."

"Classic colorless, cold bitch. She looks like she's wearing a chastity belt." Cammie snubbed out the joint and carefully put it back in her purse. "Ben will get sick of her in about five minutes."

"I don't think so," Dee said. "He seems to be really, really into her and—"

"Whose side are you on?"

"Yours, of course," Dee replied. Letting Cammie know how she felt about Ben was even more dangerous than letting Sam know. But Dee was used to covering up how she really felt about things. She just made her voice a little breathier and her eyes go really wide. Which was exactly what she did now.

"I'm not saying she's any real comp for you, Cammie," Dee added, hedging her bets. "You know that."

"Right," Cammie agreed. She giggled as the pot hit her. "Oh, yeah. I feel so much better."

"Let's go in—I really have to pee," Dee said.

"I'm not ready. Pretend you're Bambi. Go in the woods."

"That wouldn't be very sanitary, Cammie."

Cammie laughed. "You are too funny. You're worried about 'sanitary' after your last so-called boyfriend? Wasn't he the one who never wore underwear?"

"It wasn't his fault; his cleaning lady was deported."

Cammie took out her compact and looked in the mirror, fluffing up her mass of curls. "How can that washed-out blonde compare to *this*? Answer: She can't." She put her compact back in her purse. "I think it's time for a little divine intervention."

"Prayer can be really helpful, Cammie," Dee said, crossing her legs, she had to go so badly. "And I swear to God, I really have to pee."

Cammie shot her friend a withering look. "Not *prayer*," she spat. "There are three things that are truly divine, Dee: that fat transvestite who starred in all the John Waters movies; forgiveness—although that one is highly over-rated—and me, when I take Ben's bitch down."

"Everything is *so* nice," Cammie said, smiling at her tablemates. "Nice, nice, nice."

Anna felt certain that Cammie had gotten stoned in the ladies' room. Her pupils were the size of pennies, and she had a really stupid grin on her face. Of course, there was an upside: Cammie was no longer being bitchy. Frankly, Anna was happy for the respite.

"Here comes the daughter of the groom," Cammie sang out to the tune of "Here Comes the Bride." "She looks so-o-o-o pretty."

Sure enough, Sam was heading for their table, now sporting the figure-flattering black dress.

Dee smiled. "I found that dress for her. It's a size *ten*," she added significantly.

"Whatever size it is, she looks *great*," Adam said.

"Tell her that and you are so getting laid tonight, dude." Damian smirked.

There was more bitchy banter. Anna found it exhausting. And boring. Didn't Ben's friends ever talk about anything that mattered?

Ben put his hand on Anna's. "Would you like to da—"

"So, I'm dying to dance," Sam chirped as soon as she reached the table, resting her hand on the back of Ben's chair, behind his neck. "Ben?"

"Actually, I just asked Anna. Later, okay?"

"Oh, sure. Okay. That's—that's fine," Sam stammered. "I mean—"

"Hey, Sam, I'm the lonely guy without a date," Adam said, quickly getting to his feet. "Let's go." He took Sam's hand and led her toward the dance floor.

"Ooh. Shot down at her own father's wedding," Damian exclaimed as a waiter set his dinner of pistachio-encrusted salmon before him. He ignored it and reached for what looked like a glass of scotch again. "That's gotta hurt."

"You could have danced with her," Anna whispered to Ben. "I think you hurt her feelings."

Unfortunately, no one had warned Anna about Cammie's bionic hearing. "That's so sweet of you to care," Cammie oozed. "You must be a very kind person."

Anna didn't bother to respond to that; it was so obviously insincere.

"Is everybody ready to par-tay?" a deejay asked, taking over for the orchestra as they went on break. He started spinning some house music. Anna was grateful for the excuse to leave the table.

"Oh, I love this!" Cammie said gaily, jumping out of her chair. "Let's all dance."

As the others at the table rose, Ben did, too. He held out a hand to Anna, who stood up just as Cammie was passing behind her chair. Anna felt the tug on the bottom of her silk dress at the same moment she heard the sickening sound of ripping silk.

She looked down. The bottom of her dress was impaled by Cammie's right stiletto heel. Anna reached behind her . . . and hit the lacy bottom of her La Perla chemise, which barely covered the curve of her butt. The vast majority of the bottom of her dress was on the floor.

"Oh my God, what happened? Let me see!" Cammie stepped back and spun Anna around so quickly that Anna didn't have time to resist. Which meant that Cammie, her friends, and pretty much everyone at the wedding were gawking at Anna's lace-covered ass.

"Killer lingerie," Damian pronounced.

"What the hell happened?" Ben asked.

Cammie clapped her hands to her cheeks. "Oh, I'm so sorry! The bottom of your dress must have brushed the floor when you were getting up—what a terrible accident."

Anna dead-eyed her. It was no accident, and they both knew it.

"What a shame. And your dress was so gorgeous, too," Cammie went on. "I'll pay for it, of course."

Anna was careful to keep her voice steady. "I'm sure you will."

"God, you must be so embarrassed." Cammie's voice oozed sympathy.

Yes, she was. All Anna wanted to do was to walk out of the damn wedding and never have to see any of these horrid people again in her entire life. But she was Jane Percy's daughter. And she refused to let this overly made-up, over-the-top bleach job get over on her.

"Why would I be embarrassed?" Anna asked coolly. "*I'm* not the one who ruined my dress. Besides, like Damian said, I'm wearing killer lingerie."

With a look of admiration at Anna's poise, Ben removed his tux jacket and held it out. Anna slipped it on. It fell almost to midthigh, which was a relief. Then she reached for a sharp knife and cut off the bottom half of the front of her dress, still leaving it somewhat longer than the back. Adrenaline coursed through her veins. Yes! She was having a Cyn moment. No, she was having a new-and-improved Anna moment.

She laid the material on her chair, turned to Ben, and said, "Let's dance."

Twelve

Crappy Muzak serenaded Sam as she leaned her throbbing forehead against the bathroom mirror. Her evening was a disaster. Nothing was going right. How could Ben have rejected her in front of everyone when she'd asked him to dance with her? Damn that *My Big Fat Greek Wedding* piece of shit! In real life the fat girl never got the hot guy.

Thank God it had been Adam Flood to the rescue. Adam was a sweetheart. Sam had suffered through the obligatory arm-thrusting-in-the-air to "Shout," and then she'd excused herself to find privacy in the now empty observatory. There she'd called Dr. Fred, to whom her father paid a massive yearly retainer. He could damn well help Sam in her hour of need.

Only Dr. Fred hadn't. Instead he'd been incredibly irritated that Sam had called him at home on New Year's Eve. When she told him how terrible everything was, he asked her if she'd been saying her affirmations: *You are not fat. You are beautiful. You create your own universe.*

Fuck Dr. Fred and his fucking mantras, too. Like his ass wasn't the size of the San Fernando Valley.

He said he was sensing hostility.

No shit. Who did he think he was kidding with that "you create your own universe" bullshit? *She* wasn't the one who'd decided her father should marry a pregnant bimbo. *She* wasn't the one who'd told Ben to bring a gorgeous girl to the wedding. *She* wasn't the one—

Dr. Fred had interrupted to say that he'd see her at her usual time on the second and that he had to depart for a charity gala. Like Sam cared. She was in the middle of a crisis, she told him, and—

That was when the line had gone dead. He'd hung up on her! Hadn't he seen *Good Will Hunting*? He was supposed to be telling her how none of this was her fault in a really soothing Robin-Williams-when-he-wasn't-playing-psycho–type voice.

She'd pushed redial immediately. Dr. Fred had tried to run some story on her about how his kid had disconnected their call. Right. He just didn't want neurotic celebrity offspring all over Beverly Hills deleting his number from their PalmPilots. Well, too bad. She'd fired his ass.

That moment had led Sam to the ladies' room farthest from the reception so that she could be alone. Then she locked herself in a stall, took out the Valium she'd stashed in her evening bag, and popped it. Usually V took the edge off. Tonight it just intensified her misery. She couldn't think of one good thing about her shitty life. That made her cry.

Too late, she remembered that she wasn't wearing waterproof mascara. She rushed to the mirror to survey the damage. Tracks of black trailed down her cheeks. Her eyes were bloodshot. Her lipstick smeared down toward her chin. She looked like the fat has-been druggie Patty Duke played in *Valley of the Dolls,* Neely O'Hara.

Just when Sam thought things couldn't get worse, they did. The bathroom door opened, and in walked Ben's date. She was wearing Ben's tux jacket and hardly anything else. Sam momentarily forgot about her own ravaged face.

"What happened to your dress?" Sam asked.

"What happened to your face?" Anna countered.

As if there were any way in this galaxy that Sam would confide in this girl. "I got something in my eye and my makeup ran."

"Right. And I got caught in a wood chipper."

Sam sagged into one of the bathroom's velvet vanity chairs. What the hell difference did it make if she told the truth? "I cried my makeup off," she confessed. "Now I'm totally fucked."

"My dress got torn off in front of four hundred people," Anna said, "most of them famous. Now *I'm* totally fucked, too. I was looking for an out-of-the way place to lick my wounds."

"Ditto. What happened?"

Anna explained, and Sam tried not to gloat as Anna unbuttoned Ben's jacket to reveal the jagged edges of her ruined gown. But when Anna pulled the ruined

dress over her head and threw it in the trash, Sam
seethed. That Anna's silk-and-lace chemise was stun-
ningly beautiful wasn't the problem. It was how fabu-
lous Anna looked in it that made Sam want to kill the
bitch. "Did Cammie do it on purpose?" Sam asked.

Anna put Ben's jacket back on. "What do you think?"

"Oh, yeah."

Anna shook her head. "You say that as if it's perfectly normal behavior."

"Well, for her it is."

"And she's your friend?"

Sam shrugged. "Mine, not yours. Which means she'd
kill for me. She'd even kill *you* for me, that's how good
a friend she is."

"I hope you mean that metaphorically and not literally," Anna said.

And she's educated, too, Sam thought. Like it could
get any worse.

"Actually . . ." Anna rummaged around and held up a
small tube. "Elizabeth Arden Eight Hour Cream. I use
it for lip gloss. But it will take off anything."

"Oh my God, you just saved my life. Thank you."
Sam plucked some tissues from a brocade box on the
counter and squeezed some of the thick ointment onto
her hand. "You know that Cammie and Ben had a thing
last year?"

"I gathered as much." Anna sat next to Sam. "But if
Ben wanted to be with her, he'd be with her."

Sam began to wipe off her ruined makeup. Ben was

supposed to be with *her*. Not Cammie. Certainly not with this wench. If only she could direct life the way she could direct a film. It could be like that loser flick *Stepmother*, only with a decent script. Anna would get one of those really gnarly diseases where her skin got all scaly and gross. That would offer pathos and also be dramatically satisfying. Then she and Ben would come together at Anna's bedside to care for her, realize that they had a magical bond, and *then* she and Ben would walk off together into the sunset . . . *with Anna's blessing.*

Sam snuck a glance at Anna. Her skin was perfection. Plus no way would Sam let her know that she wanted Ben more than she wanted a waist as tiny as the latest supermodel on the cover of *Cosmo*. Let the chick believe all she had to worry about was Cammie.

"I'm about to give you some excellent advice," Sam began, using another tissue to remove the last of her makeup. "Cammie Sheppard gets what Cammie Sheppard wants. Underestimate her at your own peril." Sam stared at her naked face in the mirror. "God, I look like shit without makeup."

"I don't think so."

"That was supposed to be sweet, right?" Sam swiveled to Anna. "Do you have any idea how obnoxious it is when a girl who really *does* look good without makeup tells a girl who looks like crap without makeup that she looks good without makeup?"

"So you think—what?—that I was patronizing you?" Anna guessed. "Or sucking up to you or something?"

"Both, probably. Pretty much everyone does."

"Why?"

Sam sighed impatiently. "No one wants to risk pissing me off."

"Because your father is Jackson Sharpe?"

"Aren't you the rocket scientist."

All the sarcasm from Sam and her friends was really starting to irritate Anna. "There are dozens of famous people here, Sam. Your father is just one more. So I don't see what the big deal is."

"All celebrities are not created equal. My father isn't just A-list. My father is A-plus-plus-plus-practically-in-his-own-stratosphere list."

"And that's what you think is important?" Anna asked.

"That's what *everyone* thinks is important."

Anna rose and headed for a stall. "I'll be sure to mention that to the starving children in Africa." She disappeared inside.

Sam's jaw hung open. Anna was amazing. What gall. Like she spent her time in sackcloth and ashes, washing the feet of the little people. Please. The pearls she was wearing alone could have fed a small country for a week.

Anna came out of the stall and washed her hands. Sam handed Anna's cream back to her. "Thanks."

"You're welcome." Anna dropped the small tube back into her purse. "I guess we should get back out there. Your father's going to wonder where you are."

"Doubtful, since I'm sure he didn't even notice that I left in the first place." Anna opened her mouth to speak, and Sam raised her palm to stop her. "Wait, don't tell me, you and your father have a perfect relationship, he worships the ground you walk on, yadda, yadda, yadda, right?"

"Hardly. He didn't even show up at the airport to meet my plane," Anna admitted.

Sam was shocked. "Really?"

Anna nodded. "I can go a year without seeing him. Maybe more."

"I know the feeling," Sam said. "What is he, an agent? Producer?"

"He's not in show business. I hardly know what he does anymore—something in finance. We aren't exactly close."

Huh. Anna didn't look like a girl *anyone* would forget, ever. Knowing that Anna had been dissed—and by her own father—perked Sam up immensely.

"That sucks," she said cheerfully. "My dad does that, too."

"Well, *no* dad should do that," Anna said. She walked to the door. "I should get back. Your friends probably think I'm in here crying my eyes out over my dress; I really hate to give Cammie that satisfaction. You coming?"

Sam turned back to the mirror. "Not with this face."

Anna pondered this for a moment. "If you have some matches, you can burn one and rub the charcoal around your eyes—it'll look like kohl. It's one of my friend Cynthia's tricks."

"That really works?"

"I've seen her do it."

Sam found some matches in her purse, lit one, blew it out, and smudged the charcoal around her eyes. "Does it look like a bruised-eyed, heroin-chic, super-model kinda thing? Or like a pathetic, insane-fat-girl-with-burnt-carbon-all-over-her-face kinda thing?"

"It looks good. Really," Anna assured her. Which pissed Sam off, because it was hard to hate someone who was nice. Sam knew so few nice people. She really did want to hate Anna. Only she didn't. It would have been great to have a friend like her.

Before Sam could stop herself, these words popped out of her mouth: "Listen, I wonder if you want to—nah, you wouldn't."

"What?"

"It's just that when you mentioned starving children . . . Tomorrow afternoon I'm going to Venice, down by the beach, to feed the homeless. It's kind of a New Year's Day ritual I do every year. I thought maybe you'd like to come and help out—I could use an extra hand. But listen, I'm sure you're all jet-lagged, and after you party all night tonight—"

"Actually, I'd like to come. I'm always looking for a reason to feel better about myself," Anna interrupted. Her brows knit together. "You do this every New Year's Day, you said?"

Sam nodded. "Why?"

"It's just . . . I misjudged you, that's all," Anna said quietly.

"Yeah, whatever. It happens." Sam jumped up from the vanity. "You know what I'd really like to do?"

"What?"

"Blow off this wedding. There's this insane New Year's Eve bash on the Warner Brothers lot tonight. We oughta go."

"'We'?"

"The people at your table. My friends." Sam pulled out her cell. "I'll call and put us all on the list. It'll be fun."

"Sam, I hesitate to point this out, but you'd be walking out on your own father's wedding."

"Like I said, he won't notice. Besides, Poppy is going to sing a medley of Broadway hits. It won't be pretty."

Anna hesitated. "Well . . ."

"Please-please-please-please-please?" Sam wheedled. "We can get wasted and watch the sun rise from the top of the WB water tower. It'll be fun."

Anna still didn't answer. For a nanosecond Sam watched herself from the outside—a pathetic girl desperate for Anna to come partying with her. Stupid, stupid, stupid, Sam thought. She is not your friend. She is your enemy. She stands between you and Ben. You hate her guts. But you still need her to like you.

"I really wasn't planning to stay out all that late tonight—" Anna began.

Sam snorted dismissively. "What are you, thirty?"

She punched a number into her cell phone. Out in the tent, at table forty-two, a cell phone rang. It belonged to wedding guest Kiki Coors, Jackson Sharpe's personal assistant. She answered it. It was Sam, wanting a phone number. Kiki looked it up on her PalmPilot and gave it to her boss's daughter.

"Where are you calling from, Sam?" Kiki asked when she noticed Sam's empty seat at the head table. But Sam had already hung up.

"Got it," Sam told Anna, punching another number into her phone. "So you'll come with me, won't you?"

"I just really can't speak for Ben—"

"Look, I know you and I got off on the wrong foot," Sam interrupted. "I was all freaked about the wedding, and I wasn't very nice to you. Please come to this party with me so that I can make it up to you. I know Ben will want to."

Anna said yes. Sam wasn't surprised, figuring that a girl like Anna was far too kind to decline an invite once she turned on the pathos.

At the party she'd figure out some way to get Ben away from her. Anna might be really nice and all that, but all was fair in love and war. Sam figured this was both.

Thirteen

As Anna walked back to the reception, she thought about Sam and was perplexed. Just when she'd been certain that Sam and company had been cast from the same mold as the three witches from *Macbeth*, Jackson Sharpe's daughter had shown her more-than-human side. Anna almost kind of sort of liked her. And she felt as if Sam almost kind of sort of liked her, too.

Los Angeles was just so bizarre.

Like the Shakespearean crones, Sam proved to be a prescient soothsayer. As predicted, a couple dozen kids were happy to ditch the wedding reception. Also as predicted, Ben was among them, though he expressed a certain disbelief that Anna would voluntarily go someplace in a group that included Cammie Sheppard. But Anna had dealt with bitches before; her private school was full of them. Same shit, different coast, she figured.

There was, however, the issue of couture. The plan was that Ben and Anna would stop at Anna's father's house so she could change clothes. But as they drove away from the party, it occurred to Anna that she really

110

didn't want to stop at her father's house. He might actually be there, in who knew what kind of state. And Anna didn't want Ben to see him like that. There was no need for Ben to see all of Anna's warts in one night.

On the other hand, she was wearing nothing but a skimpy lace chemise and Ben's jacket, and it wasn't as if there were a boutique open just for New Year's Eve shoppers, though she kept her eyes open, anyway, as Ben steered west on Sunset Boulevard.

He rounded a bend and stopped at a red light. That was when Anna realized she'd been wrong. There actually *was* one store open—a large glass-fronted place on their left. The question was, did she have the nerve?

"Pull in there," Anna said, before the saner portion of her brain could stop her. She nudged her chin in the direction of the store.

Ben's eyebrows hit his hairline. "There? Are you sure?"

God, no. "Absolutely."

"But . . . that's a sex store," Ben explained.

"I can see that," Anna agreed. "The bondage mannequins in the window are a dead giveaway." She gave him her brightest smile. "Let's go."

I am walking into Larry Flynt's world-famous *Hustler* sex emporium hand in hand with Ben Birnbaum, Anna thought. I am not self-conscious. I am fine.

Anna hoped that if she kept that litany playing in her mind, she could prevent herself from melting into a puddle of embarrassment.

"That sign says this is the largest store of its kind in America," Anna pointed out as they entered.

"You've never been to anyplace remotely like this before, have you?" Ben guessed.

"Not even close," she confessed, relieved not to pretend that she was taking all this in stride.

The *Hustler* store sold everything from anatomically correct blow-up dolls to edible massage lotions to leather dominatrix outfits. It was jammed with customers planning to usher in the New Year, each in their own special way.

Anna and Ben dodged around a couple in matching chaps looking through the porn DVDs. Anna tried not to stare as across the aisle, a woman who'd obviously had more plastic surgery than Joan Rivers was heaping rubber goods into the arms of a studly man young enough to be her grandson.

Finally they found the clothing area, such as it was. Mostly see-through nighties with matching crotchless thongs, leather bras with the centers cut out, and a large selection of dominatrix boots.

"Not exactly Bloomingdale's," Ben opined. "Not that I'd mind seeing you in any of this stuff, you understand."

"Hel-lo, I'm Carmen," said a bass-voiced black clerk as he sauntered over. Carmen's thigh-high, stiletto-heeled boots below red hot pants made him tower over both of them. He gave Ben a quick once-over. "And you, I'd *love* to help personally."

"We're fine," Anna demurred. After the he-geishas,

Anna was starting to feel as if cross-dressing was some kind of Los Angeles motif.

"I can see *that*," Carmen agreed, his eyes locked on Ben.

Ben scratched his chin. "Okay. Nothing personal, but go away."

"Well, just scream if you want me, Love Muppet. Kiss-kiss." He added a wink for Ben's benefit and sashayed off to assist other customers.

"It must be hard to get help on New Year's Eve," Anna said, trying to keep a straight face.

"No shit."

Ben looked embarrassed, which was so cute that Anna felt emboldened. "I'll make you a deal: I'll pick one thing to try if you will, too."

"I don't know . . ."

"Oh, come on," Anna coaxed, hardly believing her own audacity. She kissed him softly. "It'll be fun." She kissed him again, harder this time. One part of her was saying, "What the hell are you doing?" and another part of her was telling the first part to shut up. She felt like a snake, shedding one skin for another.

"How can I possibly say no to that?" Ben asked. "But I draw the line at wearing any of this shit out of the store."

They shook on it. After much deliberation Anna chose some low-slung, leopard-print vinyl pants that zipped all the way around from the back to the front. She slipped into a dressing room and determined through experience that actually putting them on could be hazardous to a girl's anatomy. They were very, very tight. On a whim, she rolled up the bottom of her chemise and knotted the material under her bust. Between the bottom of the chemise and the top of the pants, she was exposing more skin than she was covering. But she had to admit: she looked kind of sexy . . . in an incredibly lowbrow, sleazy sort of way. She could almost hear Cyn's applause from the other side of America.

All righty, then.

She pulled open the curtain to the dressing room and stepped onto the sales floor. What she saw made her crack up. Ben had traded his tuxedo trousers for black leather chaps. "Where's a photographer from the Princeton University newspaper when you need one?" Anna said, still laughing.

"Ha ha. I'm changing before Carmen decides to drag me home and make me his love slave. You, by the way, look fantastic."

Anna looked down at the tacky pants. "This is so not me."

"That's what makes it so hot." He kissed her lightly and returned to the dressing room. When he came out, they found Carmen. Ben paid him for Anna's pants, then Anna slipped Ben's tux jacket back over her new "outfit."

"Buh-bye," Carmen called as Ben and Anna pushed out of the store. "Hey, girlfriend? At the stroke of midnight, you ring that boy's chimes for me."

They stepped out into the brisk night. Anna had never felt so alive, so on the edge of possibility before, in her entire life.

Ring Ben's chimes, huh? Anna thought. Carmen, I might just do that.

Fourteen

Cammie was so not impressed.

The party at Warner Brothers was a fund-raiser for Artists for Peace. Celebs loved to join because it made them seem political, which made them seem smart. It was good for the image and allayed the guilt they felt over earning obscene amounts of money. Scanning the crowd, Cammie determined that this bash had turned into an event for the Hollywood A-listers (and wannabe A-listers) who, for one reason or another, hadn't been invited to Jackson Sharpe's wedding. The party had a circus theme to represent hope, and the event planners had pulled out all the stops. There were clowns, animal handlers, mimes, and even death-defying trapeze artists. In fact, intrepid guests could be harnessed up (to prevent them from falling drunkenly onto other revelers and perhaps taking out someone who might help their career) and join in the aerial act. There was even a functioning fun house.

In the center ring The Giraffes' lead singer launched the band into what sounded to Cammie like been-there-done-that retro-grunge rock 'n' roll. ("Our first single is at number five with a bullet on the R&R college radio charts. Thank you, Los Angeles!") Couldn't anyone ever have an original idea?

Lots of people evidently hadn't merited an invite to the Sharpe-Sinclair nuptials, because the ring was filled with people dancing the night away. Cammie couldn't have cared less. All she cared about was how she was going to handle things when Ben finally made his entrance with Her. Not that she'd let that show. In fact, she leaned against a tent pole, the picture of femme ennui. Nearby, Sam was staring at the entranceway, biting at a cuticle. Dee was rocking out to the music.

Parker came over to Dee. "Dance, Dee?"

"Say no, Dee," Cammie counseled.

"Why?"

"Never dance with a boy better looking than you are."

Dee reddened. "That was a mean thing to say."

"Don't pay attention to her, Dee. You're gorgeous," Parker assured her over his shoulder as he tugged Skye to the dance floor.

"Sometimes I wonder why I'm even friends with you, Cammie," Dee complained.

"You're a masochist?"

"Ha." Dee listened to the band for a while, checking out the crowd. "Do you think that guy is gay?"

"Parker? He'd do Oliver Stone on President Kennedy's eternal flame and scream, 'Conspiracy, conspiracy!' if he thought it would help his career," Cammie replied. "I

don't mean Parker." Dee edged closer. "I mean that guy
behind you."

"Is he checking you out?"

"I think so."

"Is he well dressed?" Cammie asked, still not turning.

"Very."

"Great hair, great skin?"

"Uh-huh."

"Gay." Cammie plucked a flute of champagne from a
passing waiter.

"You didn't even look!" Dee protested.

"I don't have to. One: Jackson Sharpe is a closet
homophobe, so a lot of the Hollywood gay mafia didn't
get invited to his wedding. Two: Gay guys like studio
parties—one of their few lapses in good taste. Three:
Gay guys know how to dress. Four: Gay guys care about
their hair and skin even more than we do. Five, six,
seven, and eight: Gay guys love you, even if they haven't
figured out they're gay yet. Do the math."

Dee sighed. Obviously Cammie was still irritated
that the girl with Ben had pulled off the ripped-dress
thing with such aplomb.

"Dance, Sam?" Adam appeared suddenly behind
the trio.

"Uh . . . maybe later."

Adam headed off with someone else. Cammie eyed
her friend. "He likes you, you know. Why didn't you
dance with him?"

Sam shrugged.

"Hey, how come you don't tell *her* not to dance with a guy who's better looking than she is?" Dee complained.

"Well, first of all, I was only kidding, and second of all, because you know you're cute. Sam doesn't. Why do you keep staring at the door, Sam?"

"I just want to make sure Ben and Anna are on the bouncer's list. You know how guest lists can get screwed up."

"Have you noticed how much Anna looks like that nympho in *Sorority Sisters*?" Cammie asked. *Sorority Sisters* was a B movie that Cammie had rented for a sleepover one night. "Maybe it *was* her."

"It wasn't," Sam said bluntly.

Cammie raised her eyebrows. "Are you defending her?"

"Ripping her dress off really sucked, Cammie."

Dee overheard. "It was an accident!" she insisted. "Cammie didn't do it on purpose."

"Right," Sam muttered, and bit at another cuticle. This whole situation was just nuts. Cammie was her friend, not Anna.

Suddenly Sam saw them at the door with the bouncer, who was scanning the guest list for their names. She took the moment to prepare for battle, sucking in her stomach and tousling (artfully, she hoped) her hair.

"Hey, Sammikins!"

A bald guy with an unfortunate lack of chin cut between Sam and her line of vision of Ben, instantly enveloping her in a bear hug. Ken Bertram had produced one of Sam's father's few stinker films. Once he'd had a lot of power. These days he was "Ken who?"

"I heard your dad was getting married today."

"He did." Sam edged this way and that, trying to keep an eye on Ben and Anna.

"Great. Hey, I sent a nice gift."

In other words, you weren't invited, Sam thought.

"So, the little girl is all grown up. Tell me what you've been up—"

Though she was tempted to tell Mr. Bertram to save his breath for someone who wanted to help his career out of the toilet, Sam settled for a "Can you excuse me? My friend is about to kill herself, so I really need to go."

"Oh, wow—"

Sam cut around the aging producer and headed straight for Ben and Anna. "Hey, you guys!" She hugged Anna first, then Ben. "Anna, Adam said he'd chew off his own arm if you didn't dance with him as soon as you arrived. He's right over there." She pointed vaguely toward the band and then grasped Ben's hand. "Time for that rain check you promised me. You don't mind, do you, Anna?"

"No, of course not."

"Fantastic. So, we'll find you after." She tugged Ben toward the center ring dance floor. At that moment the gods smiled upon her, because the band segued into a ballad.

"Oh, I love this song." Sam wrapped her arms around Ben's neck, which left him little choice but to slide his arms around her waist or look like a total asshole. She gazed up at him as they swayed to the music. "So, having fun?"

"Sure."

"I'm glad." Sam snuggled a little closer and closed her eyes for just a moment, pretending that Ben really was hers. Ben leaned back a bit.

"So, what have you been up to, Sam?"

"Not much. Figuring out the meaning of life, that kind of thing."

He chuckled. "That sounds like something Anna would say."

How irritating. It wasn't as if Ben really *knew* Anna. Sam's mind scrambled for something, anything, to turn the conversation away from wonderful Anna with her perfect legs and—

"Next." Cammie neatly ducked under Sam's raised arms, dislodged her friend from Ben, and slid her own arms where Sam's had just been. "Well, hello there."

"Hey!" Sam objected.

"Come on—," Ben began.

"I'd love to," Cammie purred.

Sam refused to move. "We were dancing, Cammie. In case you didn't notice."

"Yuh. I'm sorry," Cammie said. "But you really need to go wipe that black crap off your face, Sam. Seriously. You look like a football player on 'ludes."

Sam knew Cammie was psyching her out, but she couldn't help herself; she swiped at the charcoal below one of her eyes.

Ben dropped his arms and stepped out of Cammie's

embrace. "You know, why don't the two of you dance together? Tonight you'd make a great couple."

Sam felt herself flush. "Why would you say something like that?"

"You weren't exactly gracious to Anna before, Sam."

"*Me?* Not gracious?" Sam protested. "I'm nice to *everyone*."

"Come on, Sam. You called her a 'B-list slut.'"

Sam flushed. "Only because I thought she was working an angle to get into the wedding. You have to admit, it's a distinct possibility."

"No, Sam, it isn't."

"I'm sure you're right, Ben," Cammie agreed smoothly. "You always did have excellent taste in girls."

Sam whirled on Cammie. "You hate her guts. *You're* the one who stepped on her dress!"

As The Giraffes stormed into something with three chords and a headbanging beat, Ben left Cammie and Sam to argue with each other and ducked out in search of Anna. But Cammie turned and went after him. She caught up with Ben in front of the fun house and snagged his arm.

"Hey." She shook her red curls out of her eyes. "That's the first time *I* ever chased *you*. Take it as a compliment."

"Right," he said, impatient to reunite with Anna. "What's up?"

Cammie's tongue flickered over her upper lip. "I . . . I really need to tell you something."

"Okay. What?"

"Not here."

Ben frowned. "Cammie, I really don't have time to—"

"Come on." She tugged on his hand.

"Forget it, Cammie. I've got a date. Remember?"

"Ben." She lowered her eyes. When she raised them again, they were teary. "It's very important. And . . . personal. Please."

Ben hesitated. Cammie knew she had him ten seconds before he knew he'd been had. After all, Ben was a gentleman. The waterworks/groveling thing always worked with gentlemen. They were just so utterly predictable.

He held up two fingers. "Two minutes, Cammie. I mean it."

"Fine. Time me." She led him inside the fun house. It was so well soundproofed that inside they could barely hear the band. She led him down a dead end to a cocoonlike room completely lined—floor included—in crazy mirrors.

"Cammie—"

"Shhh." She put a finger to his lips and snaked her arms around his neck. Then she gave him a soft, sexy kiss that promised much more. "That's what I wanted to tell you," she whispered.

"Dammit, Cammie." He stepped away from her. But Cammie heard the ragged edge to his voice and knew that her kiss had affected him.

She moved in again, molding her body to his. "Come on, Ben. You know you want me."

He pushed her away. "Cut it out."

Ben was turning her down? The bastard was actually *turning her down?* Cammie was livid, but she didn't let it show. Instead she smiled, cool as always. "So. She's that good, Ben?"

"Not that it's any of your business, but I wouldn't know."

She barked a short laugh. "Liar."

"Think what you want. I don't really care. I like this girl. A lot. And I'm not about to blow that for a quickie with you. Now are you leaving with me, or are you staying?"

She didn't move, so he turned and stormed away. Cammie and her many images fractured by the crazy mirrors watched him depart. She could feel her throat tighten. Why did she have to care about him so much? It hurt. She gritted her teeth, refusing to give in to cheap sentiment. So Ben really cared about Anna. Well, that wouldn't last. A girl like Anna was like skim milk—you felt virtuous drinking it, but eventually you just had to have a milk shake.

Cammie knew that she was the milk shake. With whipped cream and a cherry on top.

Fifteen

"Two hours till midnight!" The Giraffes' lead singer yelled into the microphone. "Lemme see you people par-*tay!*" The band went into another hard-pounding tune. From the rooftops of buildings surrounding the circus set, silver confetti rained down on the crowd.

"This is so awesome," Adam told Anna over the cacophony. "I heard there's going to be fireworks at midnight. So, would you like to dance again?"

Anna hesitated. Adam was a truly decent guy. But she had a *date*. A date she hadn't seen in twenty minutes. Where was Ben?

"I think I'd like to just go find something to drink."

"I'll get it for you. What do you want?"

"Flat water with lime would be great."

He laughed. "It's New Year's Eve and you're not drinking?"

"Not at the moment."

"Back in a jiff. Don't move a muscle." He took off like a man on a mission.

Anna edged her way to the outside of the center ring,

still looking for Ben. The party was fun in an over-the-top kind of way, an appropriate follow-up to the over-the-top wedding. It certainly wasn't the kind of party she'd normally go to. The problem, however, was that she wasn't really having all that much fun. She and Ben had hardly spent any time alone the entire evening. Wildly attracted to him as she was, she still barely knew him.

She felt the vibration of the cell phone in her little evening purse and plucked it out, holding one finger in her ear to help her hear. "Hello?"

"Anitscyn!"

Anna couldn't hear at all. "Hold on a minute!" she yelled into the phone, and backed into a small alleyway, partially shielding herself from the band. "Again, please?"

"Anna? It's Cyn!"

"Cyn!" Hearing her best friend's voice made her feel better instantly. "Happy New Year!"

"The stroke of midnight was a blast. I wanted to catch you before your witching hour. Are we having fun yet?"

"Well, I'm at a party at Warner Brothers," Anna replied.

"Really? With?"

"His name is Ben. He goes to Princeton—I met him on the plane."

"You shameless hussy!" Cyn exclaimed, laughing. "I am so proud of you."

Anna smiled. "I'm wearing my mental WWCD bracelet. What Would Cyn Do?"

"Speaking of," Cyn said. "I didn't. With Scott."

It took Anna a moment to understand, and then her heart leaped. "No? Maybe . . . you're not ready."

"Ha! Even as we speak, I'm locked in a bathroom at this off-the-hook loft party in SoHo that is showing zero signs of ending. I'm wearing this amazing Betsy Johnson dress and the world's sexiest underwear. Think how great I'll look when Scott undresses me by the dawn's early light."

To Anna's dismay, that image still twisted her heart around. She heard a pounding noise over the phone.

"Take a hike, I'm sick in here!" she heard Cyn yell. "Anna? Some asshole is banging on the door. I'd better go."

Anna held the phone tightly. "I'm so glad you called, Cyn. Have a great time tonight!"

"You too. I miss you insanely. Hey, I hope what's-his-name turns out to be the guy of your dreams, Anna. You deserve it."

They said their good-byes, and Anna slipped her phone back into her bag. Everything was so mixed up in her mind. How could she still care whether or not Cyn had sex with Scott? And why was it that when she was with Ben, she didn't think about Scott at all?

And where the hell *was* Ben?

Suddenly she felt a tap on her shoulder. "Excuse me, but my friend and I were just saying that you are by far the best-looking woman at this party," said a bald man with a salt-and-pepper goatee, which gave him the odd appearance of having his head on upside down. He waved toward the crowd to indicate where his "friend" was.

The Cyn-making-out-with-a-middle-aged-guy-whose-name-she-never-got moment flew into Anna's head. Why couldn't she do something like that? She damn well could, if she wanted to. She looked Middle-Aged Goatee Man in the eye. And the idea of kissing him made her want to puke.

"Thanks," Anna said. "I'm flattered."

"Gerard Maxwell. I'm a producer. Call me Jerry. I'm sure you've seen some of my films."

"I don't go to the movies all that much," Anna said politely. She looked over the man's head, hoping to see Ben in the crowd. No such luck.

"No bullshit," Jerry said, stroking his goatee. "You got it going on." His gin-soaked breath wafted in Anna's direction. It was everything she could do not to wave her hand in front of her face to try to disperse the odor.

"Nice to meet you, Jerry. Excuse me, please." Anna began to edge past him.

"Wait, wait, just a second. Seriously."

Anna sighed and turned back to the man. "What?"

"I'm rich," Jerry announced.

"How nice for you," Anna said in her frostiest Jane Percy tone. "And now I really have to—"

"I just want to ask you one thing."

Anna was trying to conjure up a What Would Cyn Do–type "fuck off" when the producer leaned close and asked, "How much?"

Anna had zero idea what he was talking about. "Sorry?"

"For the night. For me and a friend. Together."

Suddenly Anna understood. And felt like a total idiot for not having caught on sooner. This boor thought she was a hooker.

"Name your price, baby," Jerry went on, raising his voice. "It's New Year's Eve, and I got the money, honey!" He pulled a fistful of bills from his pocket and waved them in Anna's face. People around them snickered.

For the first time Anna thought how slutty she must look in her ridiculous vinyl leopard pants and heels. What had been so funny and sexy with Ben was now just trashy and embarrassing.

"Come on, baby," Jerry wheedled. "That other chick told us you were up for anything."

Anna bristled. "What 'other chick'?"

"Red curls, body that won't quit?"

Anna knew instantly. Cammie Sheppard. Cammie had told this walking pond scum that she was a hooker. In the *Hustler* store outfit she was wearing, she could see how he'd believe it.

Did Cammie really think this would help her get Ben? Or was it personal now, and she just wanted to humiliate Anna one more time? It was all such a massive waste of time and energy. Maybe she should take up tae kwon do, or kickboxing, or something that would allow her to simply kick Cammie's ass so that the girl would stop playing all these mind games.

Well, no time for that now. She'd have to kick her ass mentally. WWCD?

"Tell you what." Anna dropped her voice confidentially. "You go tell the girl with the red curls and the body that won't quit that if she's in, I'm in. That is, if you can handle both of us."

Jerry grinned widely. "*Now* you're talking."

"Give her the money. She and I are very . . . close. What's mine is hers. If you know what I mean. So, we'll meet you at"—she racked her brains for the name of a Los Angeles hotel—"the bar at the Century Plaza. At midnight."

"Oh yeah, baby, I am down with that." Jerry was practically drooling as he pushed into the crowd to get back to Cammie.

Asshole. Anna hoped some flying Wallenda on the trapeze would swan dive onto the idiot's head. She took off in the opposite direction but didn't get more than thirty feet before Sam grabbed her arm.

"Where's Ben?" Sam demanded. Anna noticed that the charcoal she'd smudged around her eyes was gone.

They both heard Ben's voice. "Right here." He edged toward them, three drinks in his hands. "With refreshments."

"You mean to tell me you left Anna alone *all this time?*" Sam asked, as if Anna were her very best friend in the world.

"I'm very sorry," Ben said. "I plan to make up for it. Ready to call it a night?"

Anna snuck a look over her shoulder at Jerry, who'd been joined by a fat friend. They were now working their respective mojos on Cammie at the bar. Excellent. "I'd be happy to call it a night."

"You're leaving?" Sam asked, trying to cover her dismay. "It's not even midnight yet."

Ben kept his eyes on Anna. "There's someone I need to see."

"Funny," Anna said, staring back at him. "There's someone I need to see, too."

"But it's a party. It's New Year's Eve," Sam insisted.

"Exactly," Ben said softly. "Anna? There's someplace I'd like to take you. Someplace special. Okay?"

She nodded. "More than."

Ben gave Sam a good-night kiss on the cheek and then led Anna back toward the main entrance. Sam watched them depart, knowing there wasn't a damn thing she could do about it. By the time Adam returned with Anna's flat water with a twist of lime, he found only forlorn-looking Sam.

But Sam rallied and asked Adam to go add whiskey to the water. If she couldn't have Ben tonight, she might as well drown her sorrows with Adam. Because Sam Sharpe would be damned if she'd spend New Year's Eve, and the night of her father's wedding, without a boy to kiss at midnight.

Sixteen

Anna watched the twinkling lights of the sprawling San Fernando Valley disappear behind them as Ben powered down the 405 freeway.

"Are you going to tell me where we're going?" Anna asked.

A smile twitched at the corners of Ben's lips. "Marina del Rey."

Anna knew the area. Years ago, her father had dated a woman who lived in one of the endless high-rises between the ocean and the marina. He'd taken Anna to her penthouse for lunch. Anna remembered hating the food, hating the modern Swedish furniture in her apartment, and especially hating the woman.

"Anywhere special?" Anna probed.

"It's a surprise." Ben flicked his eyes to her, then back to the road. "I'll tell you this much: It will give us a chance to be alone and talk. Good?"

"Excellent," Anna agreed. That was what she wanted more than anything.

Twenty minutes later they turned off 405 and headed

west toward the ocean; it wasn't long before Ben found the parking lot he was looking for, near the water. They parked by a sign for a restaurant called Joe's Clam.

"We're going to a restaurant called Joe's Clam?" Anna teased.

"Patience is a virtue, my beauty." He opened Anna's door and helped her out of the car. Then, hand in hand, Ben led Anna into a sprawling marina, past dozens of sailboats and pleasure crafts. Their footsteps on the wooden planks echoed across the still waters of the inlet.

Ben paused. "This is it." He made a sweeping gesture toward a yacht that glistened in the moonlight. "Welcome to the *Nip-n-Tuck III*. Or, as I like to call it, my father's excessive plastic surgery earnings put to excellent use."

"It's nice," Anna said. The truth was, she'd been on many larger vessels. Cyn's father kept one at Amagansett that made the *Nip-n-Tuck* look like a rowboat. But Anna had never been impressed by the measure of a man's water-craft. What she cared about was the measure of the man.

She kissed Ben softly. "In fact, it's beautiful."

"He's planning to buy a bigger boat next year," Ben said. "*The Botox.*"

"I'm hoping that's a joke."

"Too true to be funny. Come on." He helped her aboard. "I want to get out on the water before midnight."

Ben began flipping switches, untying lines, lifting canvas canopies, and priming pumps. "Is there anything I can do?" Anna asked.

"Sure. Climb up top." He indicated the second level

of the vessel. "Open the green cabinet on the left side of the bridge—by the captain's wheel. You'll find a CD player and music. Pick your poison. If you're chilly, there are some fleece jackets in there, too. I'll be up in a sec."

Anna followed Ben's directions and was pleased to learn that Dr. Birnbaum's musical taste ran to classical and jazz. She selected a CD of Charlie Parker's *Bird Returns*, which seemed a perfect companion to the bracing night air and the rhythmic slap of wavelets against the hull.

To the accompaniment of Bird's complex jazz solo, she made her way to the bow and stood there, inhaling the night air. She was still there when Ben eased the *Nip-n-Tuck* out of its slip. He gently accelerated, and they cruised at no-wake speed until they were clear of the marina. Then he opened up the engines and cranked the music. Anna felt salt air whip against her skin. Behind them were Marina del Rey and Los Angeles and then the vast expanse of America . . . ending at a tiny island called Manhattan. Ahead of her, she realized, was a world of possibilities that she could not anticipate any more than she could have anticipated that she would be on this boat, with this boy, at this moment.

She turned and joined Ben at the tiller. "This is incredible," she told him.

"Glad you like it." He put an arm around her and softly kissed the back of her neck.

Anna leaned into him. "When do you go back to Princeton, Ben?"

"I don't even want to think about that now."

He was right. She needed to learn to live in the moment, Anna reminded herself. She closed her eyes and let the music wash over her. "Did you know that Charlie Parker kept live birds at Birdland, but they all died from secondhand smoke inhalation?"

"I can't say I did," Ben replied, finding a new spot on her neck to kiss.

Anna laughed at herself. "I'm a font of little-known, utterly useless knowledge. It's a curse—I remember what I read."

"Do you remember this?" Ben asked. Then he gave her the softest of kisses.

Her whole body tingled. "Yes," she whispered, her forehead against his.

"We told everyone at the party that we went to the beach the night we met," Ben said, "and watched the sun rise. Well, this was as close as I could get."

Anna was touched. "It's lovely."

"*You're* lovely."

"Even if I'm still dressed like a reject from a bad disco?"

"You'd look beautiful in anything," Ben said. "Or nothing. I'm using my imagination here."

She wondered what it would be like to be naked in front of him. Embarrassing? Thrilling? The only male she'd ever been naked in front of was her doctor, which hardly counted. Would she feel self-conscious? Or was this the boy who would finally show her what it was that everyone was always screaming about? And was she ready to find out?

She honestly did not know.

For a long time they stood together under a canopy of stars, feeling the smooth power of the engines pull them out into the Pacific and the night. Only when they were well offshore and could see the coastline all the way from Santa Monica down to Redondo Beach did Ben turn down the music and ease back on the throttle.

"So, Anna Percy," he began. "I owe you an apology."

"For what?"

"Let's start with my friends, who were incredibly nasty to you. Especially Cammie—"

"You don't have to do this, Ben."

"I want to. This isn't . . . You aren't . . ." Ben ran a hand through his hair and then sighed. "Pretty funny. Me, at a loss for words. It's like this. Cammie and I dated last year."

"I gathered."

"We broke up months ago."

"Okay."

"I have zero interest in her, Anna."

"Fine."

Ben scrunched his brows together. "Why are you being so reasonable?"

Anna turned and regarded the coastline. The lights of the marina twinkled brightly. Just to the south, she could see a jet roar west from LAX into the heavens. Out here on the water things seemed so peaceful. And she liked it that way. "I suppose I could scream and tear my hair. But honestly, this moment, being out here with you—it's too great to bother."

He folded his arms and cocked his head at her. "Or you're not that interested in my song and dance because . . . you're not all that interested."

"I'm interested," she said quietly.

"Good." Ben throttled back the engines further. The *Nip-n-Tuck* slowed, then stopped. "Feel free to move about the cabin."

Anna went to the starboard rail, which had a better view of the coastline. She held up her hair, enjoying the night air's caress on her neck. Ben joined her. Anna pictured him with Cammie; they certainly made a gorgeous couple. Then she pictured Ben making love to Cammie. She didn't like that picture at all.

"Did you love her, Ben? Cammie, I mean."

"No, never."

"Did she love you?"

"It was more a physical thing. For both of us."

She glanced at him sideways. "If you recall, that's exactly how we started. Fourteen hours ago, to be exact."

He shook his head. "It's different. Cammie is like . . . like something I had to get out of my system. She's a player. She likes it that way, believe me." He glanced at his watch. "Fifteen minutes till the new year. Want champagne?"

She shook her head. "Nothing. Everything is perfect."

"Yeah. I agree." He stared out into the inky void as a gentle swell rocked the boat. "Princeton seems really far away right now."

"Do you like it?"

"Most of the time." He grew thoughtful for a moment. "It was kind of intimidating at first. Princeton's not exactly a party school. Not unless you want to flunk out, which I don't."

"Do you think you'll go into medicine, like your dad?"

Ben made a disparaging sound in the back of his throat. "I think of my father as the *anti*–role model."

"Funny. I feel that way about my mother."

"Yeah?"

"She lives life by the book. The *This Is How We Do Things* Big Book, East Coast WASP edition. It's all just so . . . so prescribed. Such a narrow, safe, sheltered existence."

"And that's not what you want?"

"No." She looked at him sideways. "If I did, I wouldn't be here with you. Girls who live strictly by the aforementioned WASPy Big Book do not date boys named Ben Birnbaum."

"I see. I'm forbidden fruit."

"Please, I live in New York." Anna laughed. "Still, Jane Percy would not approve."

"Do we care?" Ben asked.

"We do not." She leaned her head against his shoulder. "I remember in seventh grade when I came across the phrase 'an unexamined life is not worth living' for the first time—"

"Whoa. Time out. You read Socrates in seventh grade?"

"New York prep schools do that sort of thing. Anyway, the words jumped off the page. I felt like running home and screaming it in my mother's face."

"Pretty dramatic."

Anna chuckled. "Well, I didn't actually do it. No one screams in my house. Ever. It simply 'isn't done.' But it was one of those lightbulb moments, you know? I knew I didn't want to lead an unexamined life."

"Soul searching isn't exactly on the to-do list at my house, either."

Anna thought for a moment. "We probably sound like two overprivileged brats who don't appreciate what we have."

"Hey, I appreciate what I have. I also appreciate what I don't have—a father I can respect."

A sudden breeze blew some loose hair onto Anna's cheek; she pushed it behind one ear. "Why can't you respect him?"

"Gee, where to begin?" Ben asked bitterly. "Let's see. He cheats on his wife. He cheats on his taxes. And he wastes his surgical skills on bullshit rich vanity cases." He gripped the boat's metal rail. "I'll tell you the kind of guy he really is, Anna. When I turned fourteen, he took me out for what he called 'guys' night.' We had dinner at Spago. Then we went to this apartment on the beach that he and his cronies keep—my mom doesn't know this place exists, mind you. About fifteen minutes later there's a knock on the door. In walks this drop-dead gorgeous blonde. She was my birthday present."

Anna was shocked. "You mean, he got you a prostitute?"

"Those chicks charge way too much to be called 'prostitutes.' They're 'companions.' And they'll 'companion' you wherever five hundred bucks will go, including into bed with a fourteen-year-old boy."

Anna's stomach turned over. "That's disgusting."

"I didn't exactly do dear old dad proud when I refused."

"Good for you."

"Don't give me any credit for being noble, Anna. The truth is, I was scared shitless. I don't know why I'm telling you all this—"

"I hope it's because you trust me," Anna said. "And I hope I can trust you, too."

"Does that mean you're about to share your how-I-almost-lost-my-virginity story?" he teased.

"Uh . . . I don't have one, really."

"Come on." He chuckled, then realized she wasn't joking. "You mean you're—?"

Anna nodded. "To get to 'almost,' I would've had to feel like I felt with you on the plane," she confessed, her voice low. She was blushing and glad Ben couldn't see it in the dark. "I never really felt like that before."

"I'm flattered."

"You should be." The breeze freshened; Anna crossed her arms and tucked her hands beneath the armpits of Ben's tux jacket to keep them warm.

"Back in a sec," Ben said. "I'll get you a vest."

"Ben. You can warm me up without that."

She lifted her lips to his. He kissed her. Then he *really* kissed her. Then he really, *really* kissed her. After which he did things that made her forget there was a mind attached to her body. As powerful as her feelings

for him had been on the plane, they were nothing compared to what she was feeling now. It was wonderful. It
was incendiary. It was dangerous.

Ever so gently, Ben's hand snaked under the thin silk
of her camisole.

She knew she really shouldn't . . .

And decided she didn't give a shit. Because in the
This Is How We Do Things Big Book, East Coast WASP
edition, what she was contemplating didn't have a chap-
ter. Sure, some girls who carried the book around did
It: girls who were rich, WASPy, and wild for about a
nanosecond. Then they graduated from the right
school, married the right man, and joined the Junior
League to live uneventfully ever after.

To think that only that morning, she'd been on her way
to the airport with Cynthia, wondering if moving to Los
Angeles would be the biggest mistake she'd ever made in her
life, worrying that she'd never be able to stop loving Scott
Spencer. And now here she was, on a yacht just before midnight, kissing a boy who made her feel as if pygmies were
high diving in her stomach. And south of her stomach, too.

"Anna?" His muffled voice was hoarse against her neck.

The way he said her name, she knew exactly what he
wanted. It was exactly what she wanted, too. With him.
Right now.

Before she could open her mouth to say yes, the shore-
line erupted with fireworks. Streamers of light arched skyward, splitting the night sky with silver starbursts and
golden galaxies. It was the stroke of midnight.

Anna asked herself: Do you want to talk about leading an examined life, or do you want to actually do it?

"Is there a cabin?" she whispered to Ben.

"Yes."

"Good."

Anna took Ben's hand and led him to the fire down below.

Seventeen

2:51 A.M., PST

*C*amilla Birnbaum. *Camilla Babette Birnbaum. Mrs. Ben Birnbaum.*

Cammie remembered how just last year, she'd sat cross-legged on her bed like a fifth grader and doodled variations of her fantasy future with Ben on the back of her science notebook, then crossed them all out lest anyone see. Because if anyone had seen, she would have had to kill them.

Most people thought her relationship with Ben had been just this physical thing. They'd been right. But it had been more, too. Cammie *knew* him, she was sure, in a way that no other girl had. She knew all his dark and nasty secrets. She knew how to make his fantasies come true. From what she heard, many a Beverly Hills marriage had been built on less.

That he'd gotten to her heart was a secret she kept from everyone, often even from herself. But she'd been so sure—was still so sure—that on some level Ben felt the same way she did. So why did he want to fight it?

Except there she was, offering herself to Ben on a

143

goddamn plate, for chrissake. And he'd rejected her.

Rejected *her*. She was easily the hottest girl her age in 90210 *and* 90211 and probably even 90402. But when she'd kissed him in the fun house, Ben had barely blinked. He must really care about that upper-crust Upper East Side New York bitch on his arm.

Excuse me, but the girl is practically flat. And hello, a little makeup would help. Or are cosmetics too gauche for a girl with her breeding? She probably has permanent chafe marks on her thighs from keeping them squeezed together.

A New Year's Eve fending off assholes at a back-lot Warners party hadn't been what Cammie'd had in mind for the night of Jackson Sharpe's wedding. Yet there she was, still at the party with the dregs of humanity, long after her friends had left. She'd danced, drunk too much champagne, spurned three guys who invited her to their cars to do some blow and two others who'd invited her home to do them. It wasn't that she didn't like blow, and one of the guys was actually quite tasty. But she had something important, private, and very personal to do this evening, and it didn't make a whole lot of sense to drive back to Beverly Hills and then return to this side of the hill to accomplish it.

Cammie sighed and downed the last few sips of champagne in her glass. Her plan had been to invite Ben to share this mission with her. What a joke. She blinked in the direction of the band. She was seeing double of the lead singer of . . . what the hell was the name of the band again? Something that started with a *D*, one syllable. Dick, maybe? Right. Dick. She was seeing double

Dicks. Not good. Too much champagne. She had zero desire to risk a DWI. If Ben had been with her, he could have driven. But fucking Ben was fucking someone else, somewhere else. Cammie decided she would walk.

"Hey, don't leave, baby!" some guy was calling, but Cammie gave him the finger as she walked out of the party. And kept walking. Out of the Warner Brothers lot, then east on deserted Riverside Drive. Past Disney's fucking Mickey Mouse–eared fence and the building crowned by seven gigantic stone dwarfs.

When she reached NBC Studios, Cammie removed her shoes—you'd think you'd be able to walk in twelve-hundred-dollar Blahniks—and carried the stiletto heels.

Fifteen minutes later she reached the high fence that surrounded the huge Forest Lawn Cemetery complex. Obviously the place was officially closed at this hour. Not that such a minor detail would dissuade her. It had been closed every New Year's Eve. Every New Year's Eve, she'd found a way inside.

She followed the fence up the steep hill, searching for a certain spot where the fence was in minor disrepair. When she found it, she pushed hard on the chain links until they separated from the retaining pole. The fence gave way just a few inches, enough for Cammie to slither inside.

Shit. She'd dropped one Blahnik on the far side of the fence. To hell with it. She hurled the other one over the fence in the general direction from which she had come. If the shoes were there when she came back, fine. If not, whatever.

Once she found her bearings in the dark cemetery, it was only a five-minute trek to her destination. The grounds were well manicured; the close-cropped grass tickled her soles as she walked. Almost before she knew it, she was standing at the burial plot.

"Hey, Mom," Cammie said. "Happy New Year."

Cammie took her keys from her purse and shone the attached miniflashlight on the headstone. All it bore was her mother's name, Jeanne Reit Sheppard, followed by the year of her birth and death. No inscription, no Bible passage, no "beloved mother, wife, and teacher." Nothing. Nada. Zip.

Cammie trained the flashlight on the rest of the plot, saw a bit of crabgrass that had sprouted near her feet, and cleared it away. There was a dirty straw wrapper, too, which she stuffed in her purse. Would it kill the ghouls who worked these grounds to keep them up the way they were getting paid to do?

She crouched down by the headstone, lost her balance, and stumbled to the ground. Sufficiently inebriated not to feel the cold earth under her ass, she just brought her knees to her chin and circled them with her arms. This alcohol-soaked pilgrimage had been an annual event for her since she'd turned fourteen. But she'd never been quite as wasted as she was this time. Which, she would later muse, was probably why she asked what she asked. Aloud, that is.

"Was it really an accident, Mom?"

She waited, as if she actually expected her mother to psychically contact her from beyond to tell her the truth.

"It's the part about Daddy not calling the police until the next morning that's always bugged me," Cammie went on. "He *said* he'd taken a sleeping pill. Is that really what happened? Or maybe you jumped overboard. Maybe you wanted to die. I'd just really, really like to know once and for all, Mom. Now would be a good time to tell me."

Nothing.

"I could use a little help here!" Cammie called into the darkness. "Hey, John-psychic-what's-your-face-with-the-TV-show, where are you when I really need you?"

More silence.

"Shit," Cammie mumbled. "Oh, sorry for saying *shit*, Mom. I curse a lot, which is really fucked up. It's just . . . there's this boy, Ben Birnbaum. He was my boyfriend— remember I told you about him last year? Well, he broke up with me before he went away to college. Right before he dumped me, I was planning to bring him here to meet you. Dumb idea."

Cammie sighed and rummaged through her purse. "Anyway, I brought you something from the party." She took out a small square of Belgian chocolate, wrapped in a Happy New Year! napkin, and placed it on the headstone.

"Perks of being dead: You don't have to diet anymore." She picked absentmindedly at the dirt that was now embedded in the pale green leather of her dress. "Tonight I tried to get Ben back. What a joke. I thought he really cared about me. Only he doesn't. Maybe it's genetic. You know what would really suck, Mom? If it turns out that my taste in men is as bad as yours."

Cammie wobbled onto the plot itself and lay down on her back, arms splayed. She stared up into the starry, starry night. "It's so beautiful out, Mom. I wish you could see it." Tears leaked out of Cammie's eyes and ran into her ears. "Happy fucking New Year."

Eighteen

"**H**ey, Sam!"

Sam heard Parker calling to her, but she really didn't want to answer him. She was facedown on the buttery Italian leather massage table in the meditation room (right off the Sharpes' football-field-size home gym), getting what was possibly the world's best massage from a hunk o' burning love named Giovanni. ("Only one name is needed; I am Giovanni. Now I do the massage work. But I wish to be de film star, yes?")

Sam had spotted Giovanni's studly form on the dance floor at the Warner Brothers party, dancing with some pathetic case whose bad boob job looked like two igloos molded onto her concave chest. Sam had sidled over and, after one mention of the fact that she was Jackson Sharpe's daughter, "I am Giovanni" was hers. He had masterful hands, made all the more delicious by Sam's fantasy that they were attached to Ben. And the last thing she wanted was to be interrupted.

"Sam? Seriously, I need to ask you something," Parker insisted.

149

Well, that was what she got for inviting a group of
people (some of whom she didn't even know) from the
lame-ass party to come home and party with her. Since
her father and the new Mrs. had gone straight from the
reception to their honeymoon in Barbados, Sam knew
there would be no parental objections.

Sam finally opened one bloodshot eye. "What is it,
Parker?"

"Know the aquarium in the den? Well, Nude Dude
just ate one of the fish. Now he says he feels sick. So he
wants to know if any of 'em are poisonous."

Nude Dude, a pretentious jerk who'd been a second
unit assistant director (read glorified flunky—Sam knew all
the code titles) on Jackson Sharpe's latest film, had earned
his name an hour ago when he'd walked into the Sharpe
mansion, shed all his clothes, and declared, "Let the games
begin!"

"If he turns blue, call 911," Sam decreed, and closed
her eyes again.

"You must to let all de tension go," Giovanni urged
Sam in his sexy Italian accent.

Oh, yeah. Going, going, gone. As Giovanni worked
Sam's upper back, each stroke wiped away another
memory of this misbegotten evening. It was a good
thing, too. Once Ben had departed with Anna, the night
had gone rapidly downhill. Sam had drowned her sorrows with a few whiskey and waters and sobbed awhile
on Adam Flood's shoulder. She'd blamed her morose
mood on the wedding; he'd believed her. At midnight

he'd kissed her. Then she'd met Giovanni and remembered the massage tables in the home gym. That was
when she'd decided it was time to change venues. He'd
been working on her for over an hour. It was pure bliss.

"You want I do more personal massage?" Giovanni asked.

Sam didn't even want to think about what "more
personal" meant.

"No thanks. That was heavenly, though." Sam grabbed
her robe and managed to put it on without getting up,
after which she dropped the towel that had covered her
and hopped off the table. "I should go join my friends.
You coming?"

"Of course. Giovanni is yours."

Yuh. Giovanni was starting to creep her out.

Sam found her guests in the game room, playing
drunk and stoned *American Idol* with her father's
million-dollar video equipment.

"Where's Nude Dude?" Sam asked.

"Passed out in the family room," Dee said.

"Did anyone check to make sure he's still breathing?"

"Gee, I don't know," Dee realized.

Sam turned to Giovanni. "Could you go check on
the guy in the family room, down that hall?"

"Giovanni knows, how you say, de CVR."

"CPR," Sam corrected. "Good to know. Thanks."

Giovanni took off. Dee watched appreciatively. "He's
hot."

And dumb as a box of rocks, Sam thought, which might
just make him perfect for Dee. "He's all yours," Sam said.

"Thanks!" Dee hesitated. "Is he . . . hetero? Because you know what they say about Greek guys."

"He's Italian, Dee."

"Oh. Good. I'll just go see if he needs any help, then." She trotted down the hall after Giovanni.

"Let's make apple martinis!" Skye suggested, popping up from her seat and almost falling over from whatever it was she'd already ingested.

"God, they are so last century," Damian whined. He reeled his way over to Sam. "We are in need of more alcohol."

Doubtful, but Sam pointed the way to the bar off the indoor pool, anyway. What the hell. It was New Year's Eve. Her father was totally unaware of how much alcohol he had on hand. And even if Poppy knew, she probably couldn't count that high.

The crowd tumbled into the bar, which was surrounded by glass, giving them a 360-degree view of the glittering lights of Los Angeles. Someone turned on the sound system. The Dave Matthews Band filled the air. Sam winced; that CD had to belong to Poppy—Sam wouldn't have been caught dead with it. She replaced it with a hip-hop party mix—much better.

With Damian serving as bartender, an apple-martini-versus-banana-daiquiri contest ensued. Taste-testing was done on six inches of naked flesh between where Skye's sheer Galliano shirt ended and her low-slung sequined D&G camouflage pants began.

Sam watched the crowd egging on the two guys who

were licking alcohol off Skye's stomach and felt removed from the whole scene. As far as she was concerned, this was just a variation on a film she'd seen too many times. They were young, rich Beverly Hills brats who loved to party. Like *that* was fresh. Why was she here pretending to have a good time instead of with the boy she loved? Why did she have to have such a big heart and have it be full of love for a guy who didn't love her back?

Dee and Giovanni wandered back in and informed Sam that Nude Dude was still breathing. They shared an apple martini. Then Dee stripped off her clothes, made a mad dash for the indoor pool, and jumped in. Giovanni dropped trou and followed her.

Sam couldn't help but admire Giovanni's impressive physique. But it still didn't tempt her.

Skye squealed as she bobbed underneath the man-made waterfall at the shallow end of the Olympic-size pool. Damian jumped in after her. En masse, the others shed their clothes and jumped in, too. Sam did what she always did—kept her underwear on. (Drunk as she might be, Sam wasn't about to shock her friends into sobriety with a glimpse of her full-mooned ass, where-upon she imagined they'd all scream and go running off into the night like in some kind of Freddy Krueger retro-horror flick. If that happened, she'd never be able to come out before dark in Beverly Hills again.)

Nearby, Dee seemed to have dropped Giovanni in favor of Parker—they were playing some kind of "gotcha" game under the water. Giovanni seemed to be paying a little too much attention to Damian. Sam floated on her back, feeling removed from the debauchery that surrounded her. This was not at all how she'd planned to spend this evening. How many times could you get wasted and make out with some guy you didn't really care about who didn't really care about you, either?

"Does sperm float?" Skye asked Sam, suddenly looming over her.

Sam planted her feet on the bottom of the pool. The water came up to her shoulders. "Why?"

Skye cocked her chin; Sam's eyes followed. Dee and Parker, of all people, were furiously making out in the shallow end.

Skye had come to the wedding with Parker. "Are you pissed?" Sam asked.

"Please." Skye yawned ostentatiously. "I think I'll try going gay. Guys are such shits."

Sam got out of the pool and padded into one of the heated cabanas to towel off. She wrapped herself in the cashmere robe that hung on a door hook for guests and then came out, towel-drying her hair.

"Hey, Sam." Adam loped over to her. He was completely dressed. "Listen, killer party. Thanks for the invite."

"You can stay over. Everyone else will."

"Thanks," Adam said. "But my parents are going to freak as it is." He glanced at his watch. "It's past three already."

"You're so *good*," Sam teased.

"Nah." Adam brought his face close to Sam's and whispered, "Hey, you okay? About before?"

About before? "Sure," Sam replied, even though she didn't have a clue as to what he was referring to.

"Kissing you was great, Sam," he said, his voice low so that he wouldn't be overheard. "Just wanted to tell you."

That was what he was talking about? Adam had to be the nicest, sweetest guy on the planet. So why couldn't she feel about him the way she felt about Ben?

"Thanks, Adam." She kissed him on the cheek.

"Hey, if you need me to come help you clean up tomorrow—"

"This is why God invented cleaning services," Sam said. "But thanks for offering."

Adam laughed self-consciously. "Oh yeah. Sometimes I forget. At our house *I'm* the cleaning service. So, see ya." He took off.

Sam walked over to a glass wall and looked at the glittering lights of Tinseltown. Soon it would be the first light of the New Year. Ben was out there somewhere, with someone else. Sam didn't have him. And neither did Cammie, who, for some mysterious reason, had stayed at the Warner Brothers party instead of coming over to Sam's.

No, they were both shit out of luck. Ben was with Anna. They were probably making love at that exact moment for about the tenth time. Suddenly Sam was overcome with a wish to actually *be* Anna.

But even with all of Sam's money and power, that was one wish she couldn't make come true.

Nineteen

"Here lies Anna Percy, who died with her virginity intact." Anna pulled the quilt over her face so that she wouldn't have to see Ben's reaction.

"Anna, it's okay. I told you." Ben gently tugged the quilt off her face. Propped up on one elbow, he looked down at her. "If you're not ready—"

"It's not that I'm not ready. I mean, my body is ready." She puffed air between her lips. "God, this is going to sound like such a cliché: We just met. And I always imagined that the first time would be . . . not that this isn't special, because it is; it's just . . ."

Ben smiled tenderly. "The articulate Miss Percy is at a loss for words. Well, that has to count for something." He kissed Anna on the forehead. "Look, I'm a big boy. I'm not going to spontaneously combust just because we didn't do what we almost did. Okay?"

"Okay."

"But when you're ready, I'm ready."

"Okay."

He nodded, waiting a long beat. "Ready now?"

Anna burst out laughing and bopped him with the pillow. He bopped her back, then threw the pillow down to the end of the bed and kissed her softly. "No need for you to get up yet. I'll go up top and head us back to the marina."

Ben got up and unselfconsciously put his clothes back on. Anna couldn't help but admire his body. She watched as he loped up the steps and out of the cabin, then nuzzled under the quilt and pondered what had almost been.

She'd been so sure that this was the boy and the moment. And then, just as push came to shove, so to speak, she'd stopped him. Something in her gut told her this: If Ben was The One, it was worth waiting for, and if it turned out he wasn't, then she'd be very glad that she hadn't succumbed to the lust of the moment.

Or was that horribly old-fashioned? Sometimes Anna's own longing for romantic love embarrassed her. Perhaps it was reading all those nineteenth-century British novels in middle school. After she was supposed to be asleep, she used to sneak a flashlight under the covers and read until her eyes burned with exhaustion. When she fell asleep, she'd dream that she was Elizabeth Bennet, pining for her own Mr. Darcy, convention be damned.

But all that was so passé. None of the girls she knew attached much feeling to love. It was all about "hooking up." How she felt was probably ridiculous and infantile. It certainly didn't fit in with her concept of the new, improved Anna. But she couldn't help it. She'd heard so many horror stories about first sexual experiences, it made her wary.

Her sister, Susan, for example: She'd been in East Hampton at the mansion of a composer who had been deported for importing cocaine from his native Bolivia. The mansion had been left to his ex-wife. The ex-wife often encouraged her teenage son to invite his friends to swim in their pool. Then she'd select a boy for a guided tour of a lot more than her home.

Even at age fourteen, Susan's drinking problem had already been in full, albeit secret, swing. The divorcée's bar was always stocked with iced Stoli. Feeling no pain one afternoon, Susan had shed both her bikini and her virginity with one of the boys the divorcée had passed over. In other words, her sister had been the consolation prize.

Recalling that story made Anna want to cry; she made a mental note to call Susan first thing in the morning. Maybe Susan's horror story had made her even more skittish; she wasn't sure. As Anna lay there, she had no idea whether or not she'd done the right thing. Part of her wished Ben would come running down the stairs and take her into his arms, whereupon she'd be swept away by a passion she'd be unable to resist. And part of her . . . well . . . didn't.

Anna sank against the pillows and closed her eyes. Up top, she could hear Ben puttering around, swabbing the deck and replacing the tarpaulins he'd removed before. It was such a comfortable bed, the silk sheets, the down comforter, the gentle rocking of the boat. And she was so tired. . . .

"Hey, sleepyhead."

Anna opened her eyes. It took her a moment to recall where she was and why. "I guess I fell asleep," she said groggily. "What time is it?"

"Around three. I hate to wake you, but I'm going to get the car and bring it over the slip. You get dressed; I'll come back and get you."

"It won't take me long to dress," Anna protested. "I can come with you."

Ben grinned. "Nah. Take your time. I like to think of you in here, looking like you look right now. Back in a flash."

Anna got up, washed as best she could in the cabin's small basin, and quickly dressed. She felt slightly ridiculous as she pulled back on the vinyl pants, silk chemise, and Ben's tuxedo jacket. She shivered. Ben was right. It had gotten cold. And she didn't feel like searching for a fleece jacket. She decided to crawl back under the covers and wait for Ben to return with the car.

She awoke with a start. How long had she been asleep? "Ben?"

No answer.

"Ben?" Louder this time.

Still no answer. She got out of bed and went up top.

"Ben! Where are you?" Up on the deck, she could read her watch. The time made her stomach lurch. It was almost four o'clock in the morning. Ben had departed for the car a little after three. So where was he?

"Ben!" Her voice echoed across the deserted marina.

"Shut the hell up, we're trying to sleep!" someone bellowed from another boat.

Anna climbed off the *Nip-n-Tuck* and onto the dock, her heart racing. She jogged along the wooden dock, heading toward the main part of the marina. Where had they parked? Why hadn't she paid more attention? Thoughts of what could have happened to Ben slammed through her head at breakneck speed. He'd had an accident, hit his head and fallen in the water. He'd been kidnapped. He'd—

She stopped. There was the sign for Joe's Clam restaurant, with the arrow pointing toward the bar. It was the only sign like it. This was where they had parked. But the area was now deserted. No Maserati convertible. Just black asphalt and two white painted lines that framed the awful truth.

Could everything he'd told her have been a lie, an elaborate game to get into her pants? Or was he just really pissed off—after all the time he'd invested—that she hadn't put out? Pissed off enough to simply ditch her, all alone at a marina at four o'clock in the morning?

Oh my God. Would he really do something like that?

She didn't know. She couldn't think straight.

All she knew was this: Ben was gone.

Twenty

Anna leaned wearily against the Joe's Clam sign. Her shoulders sagged; she felt like crying. But even though Ben wasn't around to see her despair, she refused to give the bastard that satisfaction. She couldn't quite wrap her mind around what he'd done to her. It was just so calculated.

To think that, just an hour or so ago she'd been feeling sorry for the pathetic way Susan had lost her virginity. Now her own story struck her as even more pitiful. So she hadn't actually had sex with Ben, so what? She'd believed every lie he'd fed her. At least Susan had had no illusion that she cared about the boy involved or that he cared about her. But Anna had really thought that she and Ben were . . .

Goddamn him. Goddamn him to hell. What had made him think that she'd fall into bed with him? Or devise his elaborate lure to have her fall for him?

"Gee, do you think it might have been the fact that you practically did it with him on an airplane an hour after you met him?" she asked herself aloud.

She felt nauseated. How, how could she have been so

161

stupid? Something had to be seriously wrong with her. First she fell for Scott Spencer, a guy who didn't even seem to recognize that she was an anatomically correct female. Then she fell for Ben Birnbaum, a guy who lied his ass off just to get into her faux leopard pants.

Anna looked around the deserted parking lot, which made her New York instincts kick in. Not a good place for a girl to be alone. She knew she had to do something— but what? Call her father? That was laughable. The man couldn't make it to the airport or to lunch, so it wasn't very likely that he'd come halfway across the city to fetch her in the middle of the night. Besides, she'd have to explain what she was doing at the marina at four o'clock in the morning. Alone.

She could call a cab. But there was something sordid about taxiing home in her stupid hooker outfit at the end of the world's worst New Year's Eve. Still, what option did she have?

And then she remembered her father's driver. Django. He'd given her his business card. She'd put it in her wallet. So maybe she still . . .

She rummaged around in her Chanel clutch. There it was. She punched his number into her cell. It rang and rang.

"Yeah?" came a groggy male voice.

"Django? I'm so sorry to wake you. It's Anna."

"Anna . . ." Her name was said as if he were rifling through a mental Rolodex. "Oh, *Anna!* Hey! Happy New Year. What's up?"

"I know it's very late. The thing is . . . I'm in Marina del Rey. Near Joe's Clam bar. And . . . I need a ride home. I know it's a lot to ask; I can call a taxi if—"

"Anna," he interrupted.

"Yes?"

"I'm already there."

Anna sat in the front seat of Django's old Nissan Sentra as he powered the car down the nearly empty streets, staying alert for drunken revelers. Thankfully, he hadn't commented on her stupid outfit. Nor had he tried to make small talk or even asked what she was doing alone in the marina at four in the morning. He'd just played one of his jazz CDs and kept his mouth shut, two things for which Anna was very grateful.

They turned off Santa Monica Boulevard onto North Foothill Drive. Anna faced him. "I want to thank you for doing this."

"Don't give it no nevermind," he drawled.

"I hope you don't have a long drive home from here."

He turned up her father's driveway. "Nope. I live close."

"Oh. That's good."

"Right there, actually." He pointed past the main house to the guest house out back. When Anna was little, her grandmother had let her use that house as a life-size domicile for her dolls. But she hadn't been inside it in years.

So her father's chauffeur lived on the premises. It struck her as odd, but she was too tired to care. She rubbed her pounding temples. "I feel like I've spent the last twenty hours going the wrong way through the looking glass."

"Sometimes you're the windshield, sometimes you're the bug." He shut down the car, got out, and came around to open Anna's door for her. As she swung her legs out, her knee bumped the glove compartment. It sprang open. A jumble of CDs, photos, and papers fell onto her lap and then tumbled to the floor.

"I'm so sorry. I must really be exhausted," Anna said as she gathered the things up.

"No, I'll get them—"

"I don't mind—"

"I said, I'll *get* it."

Something in Django's tone made Anna step away from the car and let him retrieve the fallen things. But she was still holding the one thing she had settled on her lap, an old photograph. As Django rooted around on the car floor, Anna looked at the picture. It featured a little boy with dark hair, standing by a grand piano. There was a full adult orchestra behind him; a tall, silver-haired conductor stood next to the boy, one arm proudly around him. The boy and the conductor were both in black tie.

Anna drew in a quick breath when she recognized the conductor, one of the most famous conductors and composers of the late twentieth century. He was beaming at the boy, who was obviously being wildly applauded by both audience and orchestra.

Anna looked from the photograph to Django, who was still retrieving things from the floor. There was no doubt: Anna could see the boy in the man. It was Django. But when she wordlessly handed him the photo, her eyes betrayed nothing.

Everyone has secrets, she thought. No one ever really knows anyone.

Django stuffed his papers back in the glove compartment and slammed it shut. "Got everything now?"

"Yes. Thank you, Django. More than you know. I had the ultimate squished-bug kind of night."

Django scratched his stubbly chin. "Would you buy it if I told you that it's always darkest before the dawn? Or that there's a light at the end of the tunnel? Course there's always a possibility that it's an oncoming train. But still."

She mustered a smile. "Thank you for trying to cheer me up. Thank you for everything. Really. You're a gentleman and a scholar."

He nodded, shoved his hands deep into his pockets, and headed for the guest house. Then spun back to her. "Spain. Chick Corea."

"Pardon?"

"When I feel like I'm peelin' myself off the windshield, that's what I listen to. If you want to borrow the CD, drop by. Anytime. 'Night." Django doffed his imaginary hat and strode off.

Anna watched him depart, then went to the front door and opened it, thinking how good it would be to get horizontal . . . alone. And to shower. A really, really hot shower to wash away any memory of Ben Birnbaum.

She stepped into the pitch-black foyer.

A woman screamed.

Anna jumped back instinctively, her arm sweeping against the Ming vase on the small armoire near the door. It crashed to the marble-tiled floor.

The foyer light snapped on. A barefoot blonde in a blue silk robe was carrying a plate of crème brûlée cookies from Spago—Anna knew what they were because her dad sent her a pound of them every year on her birthday—they were his favorite dessert in the world. That Anna found them too rich seemed to be completely lost on him.

"What the hell was that?" Anna's father came out of his bedroom, shirtless and in pajama bottoms. He made it halfway down the stairs before he took in the tableau in the hallway. "Well. That's not exactly the way I'd planned to have you two meet."

"I'm sorry," the blonde told Anna. "You startled me."

Anna was more than startled. Not so much that this woman was obviously her father's significant other (at least for the evening), but rather because instead of what Anna might have expected—some early-twenties, over-the-top *Maxim* babe with pneumatic body parts that could double as flotation devices—this woman was tall, angular, and very thin. With the same understated blond beauty and patrician features as Anna's mother.

"It's okay, Margaret, it's my daughter," Jonathan Percy called out as he came the rest of the way downstairs.

"Yes, I gathered that," the woman said. She put the plate of cookies on the armoire. "Hello. I'm Margaret

Cunningham. It's a pleasure to meet you. Your father has told me so much about you."

Okay, this was deeply bizarre. The closer Anna got, the more this woman looked like Jane Percy's doppelganger. But Anna's good manners automatically kicked in, and she took the woman's hand. "Happy New Year, Margaret."

"So, you two." Her father's voice was hearty. "Now that we're all together and no one is going to get robbed, why don't we take that dessert and all go eat it in the kitchen? I'll make us some tea."

Tea? Anna couldn't believe her father was even making the suggestion. She glanced at Margaret, whose incredulous expression was equally reminiscent of how her mother would react.

"I'm not sure that's the best of notions right now, Jonathan," Margaret said.

"I agree." Anna hurried back up the stairs. "I'm sorry about the vase, Dad, and about the interruption. Now, if you'll excuse me—"

"Anna, wait."

"Tomorrow," Anna called back over her shoulder. "Good night." "But Anna—"

"Good *night*."

Anna made the shower as steamy as she could stand it and scrubbed herself with a loofah. Washed her hair twice. Then soaped herself again. But even with her skin red and raw, she still felt him, still tasted him. Damn Ben. Damn him to hell.

By the time she emerged from the shower, Anna felt woozy. She dried off, donned her favorite Ralph Lauren silk pajamas, and padded back to her room, more than ready to bring this insane day to a close.

It was not to be. She had a visitor: her father, now clad in jeans and a T-shirt. He was waiting for her on the antique chaise longue by the picture window.

"Anna, we have to talk."

Anna nearly groaned. "Dad—"

"Jonathan," he corrected.

"*Whatever.* It's almost five o'clock in the morning."

"We need to hash this out."

"Can't it wait until tomorrow—later today—please?"

"I don't think it can."

Anna tried to keep her voice from wavering. "I'm just not up for a talk right now. I've had a really long day. And a really awful night."

"I'm sorry to hear that."

"Me too. Which is why all I want to do is—"

"I won't be able to sleep with all this tension between us. There are things that need to be said."

Oh, poor baby. He wouldn't be able to sleep. Suddenly Anna couldn't take it anymore. Every awful moment of the past twenty-four hours came bubbling up in her like some kind of bilious sulfur spring.

"Maybe there are things that need to be said, Dad. But you could have said them when you picked me up at the airport. Oh, wait, you didn't show up for that. Well, when you met me for lunch, then. Oops. Didn't show up for that one, either. Or when I came home this afternoon and found you passed out in the gazebo—"

"I understand that you're angry."

"I'm also exhausted. I don't think either condition is conducive to a father-daughter bonding moment."

"It's awfully harsh of you to judge before you know the facts."

"What I just said *are* the facts. You stood me up, Dad."

As she pulled down the silk comforter on her bed, she mentally added: Oh, by the way, Dad—I got dumped tonight by a boy who pretended that he thought I was a precious diamond and then threw me away like so much cubic zirconia when I wouldn't put out. And it hurts. It really hurts.

Not that she'd *ever* tell him that part. But what would it be like to have a father who cared enough to ask her what had made the night so horrible? Or to feel close enough to him to want to tell him? Was it really too much to ask for?

"From your point of view, I stood you up," her father agreed. "But you never bothered to ask me what happened or why—"

"You're supposed to be the father here." She got into bed.

"Have you thought at all about what it's like for me to suddenly have you back in my life?"

Anna felt as if she'd been punched in the gut. "I thought you invited me. I'll go back to New York in the morning, if that's what you want."

"No, that's not what I want. Why are you making this so difficult?"

Anna pressed her lips together in a thin line. "Just forget it."

"No. Jeez, you're just as touchy as your mother. What I'm trying to say—if you could manage to remove that chip from your shoulder for just a second—is that I'm glad you came."

Meaningless. His words were just so empty and meaningless. Anna folded her arms and dead-eyed him. For a long moment neither spoke.

Finally her father spread his hands. "Anna, did you expect me to morph into Superdad overnight?"

Anna jutted her chin upward. "No. I don't expect anything from you at all."

"There's that attitude again. Just like your mother."

"Well, evidently you like her enough to pick her double as your playmate!" Anna exploded.

Jonathan furrowed his eyebrows. "What are you talking about?"

"I'm sure the fact that Margaret looks just like Mom isn't lost on you."

He looked shocked. "Anna, she doesn't look anything like your mother."

"You're joking. Of course she does."

Her father shook his head. "Honestly, Anna, you're so exhausted that either you're hallucinating or delusional."

"Fine. I'm wrong. You're right. She looks like a hobbit. She looks like the Velveteen Rabbit. She looks like J. Alfred

Prufrock—take your pick. Glad that's settled. And now I am going to sleep." She pulled the covers up to her chin, desperate for this day to finally—*finally!*—come to an end.

Her father regarded her for a moment. His eyes went hazy. "I didn't want it to be like this. This isn't how I . . ."

He sighed. Then he came over to the bed and gently tucked the comforter around her. It took Anna back to a time long ago, when her parents were still married to each other. On the rare night that her father came home while she was still awake, he'd come to her room to make sure she was tucked in and her reading lamp was out. He'd kiss her forehead and then go check on Susan. Anna recalled how cherished she'd felt, how loved. And for that moment all was right with the world.

The long-forgotten memory made a place behind Anna's eyes ache. With that ache came the title of a Robert Frost poem, the first she'd ever memorized: "Nothing Gold Can Stay."

Twenty-one

The young man stood by the front door of the house off North Foothill Drive, talking into his cell phone. "Yeah, I knocked, but no one answered."

"Did you ring the bell?"

"Yeah. Maybe it's broken."

"Did you consider knocking *loudly?*" Sam asked him.

"If I knock any louder, I'll, like, wake people up."

"That's the whole point, Monty," she said with exaggerated patience. "If you don't wake her up, she won't know you're there. Which means that you're like a tree falling in the forest with no one to notice that you've fallen. Which means that you don't actually exist. Which leads directly to an existential black hole. And we don't want to go there when the New Year is only eleven hours old, do we?"

"Sure don't," Monty agreed.

"Great. So knock hard and call me back."

"Gotcha." Monty Pinelli put away his cell, pounded hard on the front door, kicked it a few times, and then pounded it again for good measure. Whatever Sam Sharpe

172

told him to do, he'd do, because Sam Sharpe was his ticket.

The fact that Monty and his older brother, Parker, even knew Sam Sharpe was due to their mother, Patti Pinelli, who made sure that whatever piece of shit apartment they were living in hung on to the tattered fringes of the Beverly Hills 90210 zip code. "No one has to know exactly where you live," she always said. "Let them think you're one of them and make the contacts you need. That's how I did it."

Contacts were how Monty and Parker's mom had gotten her first—and only—film role, in an R-rated piece of crap called *Posers,* about two young models and what they did for love. The other actress had gone on to fame, fortune, and the Hollywood A-list. Patti had never gotten within flirting distance of it. She had, however, flirted heavily with Bruno Pinelli, who owned the club where she'd worked as an exotic dancer. Bruno had promised he'd use his "Hollywood connections" to help further her career. Four years and two kids later she divorced his ass, which was why Monty only knew his father by legend as "that sonofabitch."

It was right around that time, Monty was pretty sure, when his mom had first been diagnosed with clinical manic depression, a diagnosis she considered to be utter crap. The way she looked at it—she was poor, broke, had two kids, and her looks were going—there would be something wrong with her if she *wasn't* depressed.

Monty knew that he and Parker had something their mother lacked: game. Whereas she reeked of working class, desperation, and sales at JC Penney, Monty and Parker had perfected the art of the blend. They were chameleons who could change their striations to match their background. Yep, the Pinelli boys could hang with, even thrive amongst, the rich and the famous.

This was key because Monty's mom never kept them in one place for very long. Every so often his mom would stop taking her meds. Then she'd get a sudden insight: The neighbors and/or her former *Posers* costar had hired a hit man to kill her; life was a dark hole and they'd all be better off dead. That would lead her to conclude that the only way to bring herself out of this funk would be to go on an immediate shopping spree, preferably at Neiman Marcus.

She'd head for the nearest upscale mall, where she'd lift some rich bitch's wallet and use the credit cards to buy anything her heart desired. Accomplished grifter that she was, Monty's mom would then move her kids to a new place with a good school system, always one step ahead of the law.

But now Patti had told her sons that she was determined her boys would stay in Beverly Hills, no matter what it took. Parker believed her. Monty didn't. But then, Monty hardly ever agreed with his brother about anything.

Parker, who had been so named because he'd been conceived atop a Monopoly board, was a high school senior. He'd been such a cute baby that people would stop to try and lift him from his stroller in order to get a closer look. At age almost eighteen, he bore a striking resemblance to

James Dean, except he was nearly six feet tall. He culti-
vated this resemblance to the max. Like Dean, he planned
to become a movie star at a very young age. Unlike Dean,
he planned to live long enough to enjoy it.

Parker had already acquired an agent, albeit one in
the San Fernando Valley. While Parker had James
Dean's looks, Monty knew the truth: His big bro had
zero talent. His acting deeply sucked. But he had so
much personal charisma that people (read: women and
gay men and the dried-up prune who taught drama at
Beverly Hills High, who kept casting Parker in the
leads of the school plays) often overlooked that fact.

Parker's "agent" was a lascivious older gentleman
who liked Parker to do odd jobs around his ranch in
Santa Barbara. The old geezer never touched Parker.
But just the way he looked at Parker—it was enough to
make Monty sick. So he'd never gone again.

Monty (Montana, actually; Patti had been certain
that the next generation of movie stars would be named
for states of the Union) was a year younger than his
brother. Unfortunately, he'd inherited the short,
swarthy, large-beaked looks of his long-gone father. He
figured out early on that looks were definitely not
going to be his ticket; he'd have to find another reason
to make A-list kids want to hang with him. Being the
kind of guy who wanted to cover all his bases, Monty
came up with three: He was willing to be their toadie.
He was full of boundless energy and was always up for
anything. He had a wicked sense of humor.

In other words, he would do their shit work, crack them up, and keep them up all night having fun. It was a winning combination. That Monty, only a junior, was smarter than the brightest of the A-list seniors was something he kept under wraps. He knew he was much better off having them underestimate him. He had to be particularly careful around Sam, because Sammikins was almost as smart as she was insecure. Monty did not want her to feel threatened. Yet. So for now, he played the affable chump.

Today, Samantha Sharpe's flunky. Tomorrow, his own production company. One day—the world. Then all of these Beverly Hills brats could kiss his olive-skinned ass. One day, when his big brother Parker was old, ugly, and gumming his food in the William Shatner Home for the Aged, Monty might send him a nice care package of adult diapers and denture adhesive.

Sweet.

For a long time Anna thought the pounding was coming from inside her head. When she finally half opened her eyes, she realized that someone outside was banging on the front door. Evidently her father slept with earplugs, because no one was answering. The clock radio read eleven-thirty.

The banging continued; Anna rose wearily, wrapped herself in her Burberry cashmere bathrobe, and padded downstairs. She peered through the peephole of the front door and got a fish-eye view of a short guy in a baseball cap, with dark hair and a nose too large for his narrow face.

The guy stopped his knocking for a moment and listened. When he heard nothing, he started banging on the door again. Whoever he was, he wasn't giving up. But Anna was a New Yorker; she wasn't about to open the front door to a total stranger. "Can I help you?" she shouted.

"If you're Anna Percy, I have a message for you."

Anna's first thought: Ben! She swung open the door. "Yes?"

"You're Anna Percy?"

"Yes."

"What's the meaning of life?"

Anna blinked. "Excuse me?"

"Just wondered if you knew."

"Did Ben Birnbaum send you?"

"Nope." Monty handed her his cell.

Anna took it and held it to her ear. "Well?" came an impatient female voice from the other end.

"Who is this?" Anna asked, her voice still smoky from sleep.

"It's me. Sam."

Anna's mind was still only half functioning. "Sam who?"

"Hel-*lo?* You were a last-minute uninvited guest at my father's wedding? You got your dress ripped in half? I invited you to a party at Warner Brothers?"

Sam Sharpe? Why would Sam Sharpe send this guy to wake her up? Anna cleared her throat. "Right. Sam. What can I do for you?"

"Is there a short guy with dark hair and a honker the size of J.Lo's ass with you right now?"

"Um . . . yes."

"His name is Monty. I sent him to pick you up. Don't thank me; that's just the kind of bitch I am."

Anna wasn't processing. Nor did she want to process. "I'm sorry, Sam, but I just woke up. If you could call later—"

"Late night with Ben, huh?"

Ben. It all came flooding back to her. He was the last person Anna wanted to talk about or even think about. And she certainly wasn't about to talk about him to Sam.

"If we could talk later, Sam—"

"Fine. But I didn't think you were like that."

"Like what?"

"You said you'd come. To Venice Beach, to help feed the homeless?" Sam reminded her.

Now Anna remembered. "I'm so sorry, Sam. I completely forgot—"

"Yuh, that's fairly obvious. Too much Ben on the brain."

"It's not that. I just got to bed really late—"

"Fine, blow me off. I'll send your regards to the little people."

"Sam, would you stop? I have a splitting headache. But I'll come."

"How *magnanimous* of you."

"What I mean is, I *want* to come," Anna insisted, rubbing the pounding spot between her eyebrows. "Where do I—"

"Good, see ya." The cell went dead. Nonplussed, Anna handed it back to the guy, who was waiting with a cheerful look on his face.

"So, what's up?" he asked her.

"I guess we're going . . . wherever Sam is. Just give me five minutes to get dressed."

Twenty-two

11:32 A.M., PST

Anna washed her face, brushed her teeth, and threw on some jeans, a T-shirt, and an ancient gray cashmere sweater with moth holes in the sleeves. She ran a brush through her hair and pulled it into a ponytail. Then she stuck last night's evening bag into her larger Coach handbag and hurried back downstairs.

A rumble in her stomach reminded her that she hadn't really eaten since the previous afternoon's sandwich with her dad, so she made a quick pit stop in the kitchen, where she found a scrawled note from her father on the kitchen counter.

> *Anna,*
>
> *Hope you slept well. Needed to let you know that there's a snag with the internship thing. Still hope to work it out. Let's talk later.*
>
> *—Jonathan*

A snag with the internship thing?? Couldn't her father follow through on anything, ever? If it fell through, she was going to kill him; it was that simple.

She yanked the refrigerator door open angrily and found it nearly empty, except for the last of the crème brûlée cookies—so much for the help keeping the larder stocked. She grabbed a lemon yogurt, stuck it and a tea-spoon in her purse, and went out to Monty's SUV.

"Impressive," Monty said, starting the engine. He looked at his wristwatch. "Six minutes and thirty sec-onds." He looked at the yogurt in her hand and laughed.

"What?" Anna asked.

"Look behind you."

Anna craned around to see that the entire back of the SUV was filled with food: giant plastic bags of croissants and dinner rolls, huge aluminum foil trays covered in plastic wrap, filled with steak and chicken and a rack of lamb. There was a massive tray of hors d'oeuvres—mini–spinach soufflés, bite-size Reuben sandwiches, and a massive bowl of guacamole.

"I've been picking up leftovers from various New Year's Eve bashes for the past two hours," Monty explained. "Those homeless are gonna eat like kings today."

"It's great that it's not going to waste," Anna said.

Monty started the SUV. "Kinda makes you want to chuck the yogurt, huh?"

"That food's a little rich for breakfast." Anna spooned lemon yogurt into her mouth while Monty told her about Beverly Hills High. Not that she'd asked. Not that she cared, except in the sense that she was thrilled not to be going there.

Traffic was light for once—most people were probably still hung over from New Year's Eve, Anna figured—and they made it to Venice in twenty minutes. It wasn't even hard to find a parking spot close to the beach.

Monty opened the hatchback of the SUV and unloaded a cart, which he began heaping with trays of food. "So, my brother said he met you last night at Sam's dad's wedding. Parker Pinelli?"

"We sat at the same table. Were you there?"

"Had to bow out. My mom was a little under the weather, so I stayed home with her." He reached for a massive tray of pistachio-encrusted salmon that looked suspiciously like leftovers from the Jackson & Poppy nuptials. "So, you wanna hear about Venice while I work like a dog?"

"I've been here before." Anna began helping Monty unload the food. "There are canals that were built to look like Venice, Italy. I must have read that somewhere once."

"Jim Morrison lived in a house on the canal in the sixties; did you know that?"

"No." Anna reached for the chilled bowl of guacamole and balanced it on top of the salmon.

"Of course, back then the houses on the canals were funky. That's gone the way of vinyl records. Gotta have the megabucks to live in one of those cribs now." He lifted an immense vat of pâté on top of everything else on the luggage cart, then wiped the sweat from his forehead with the back of his arm. The SUV was empty. "You didn't have to help, you know."

"I was supposed to just stand here and let you do all the work?"

"That's how it usually goes. Anyway, thanks."

"You're welcome."

"All righty. Time to go party with the unfortunates!"

Monty carefully rolled the food toward the beach with Anna trotting alongside, watching for fallout. He seemed like such a nice, cheerful guy. She couldn't understand why he was surprised that she'd help him and why no one else was.

"It's about time!" Sam called, waving them over as they rounded the corner.

Wearing oversized sunglasses, with her hair tied up in an artfully messy bun, Sam was standing by a long banquet table covered with a pristine white tablecloth. Plastic cutlery, napkins, and paper plates were stacked at one end. Unfortunately, from Anna's point of view, at the other end stood Dee and Cammie.

Anna was monumentally confused. It was one thing to underestimate Sam's desire to do charity work. Dee she really didn't know at all, other than that she didn't seem that bright. But *Cammie* the Bitch? Up and at 'em on New Year's Day to do *charity work?* Something just did not compute. Anna could see from the looks on Cammie and Dee's faces that they were as surprised to see her as she was to see them.

Sam, on the other hand, found herself ridiculously happy to see Anna. At the same time, seeing Anna looking serene and slender in her simple jeans and sweater made Sam adjust the bottom of her Asian-inspired, mandarin-collared pink Roberto Cavalli shirt to make sure it covered her loathed hips. Anna had no hips. Sam would have been happy to loan her about six inches' worth. She wondered what it would be like to look like Anna. No, that was a little too *Single White Female* for her.

Dee scurried over to Sam. "What is *she* doing here?"

"Anna? I invited her."

"But *why?*"

"Because she's my new best friend," Sam said.

Dee got wide-eyed. "Really? After all the years we've been best friends?"

"Kidding, Dee."

"Oh. So then . . . ?"

Sam went for the easiest lie she could think of. "I invited her because I thought we could pump her about what she did last night. With Ben. You know."

Dee furrowed the perfect blond brows that she had groomed once a month at Valerie's. "Why do you care what she did last night?"

"For *Cammie*," Sam hastily added.

"Right. For Cammie." Dee looked at Cammie over her shoulder. "But Cammie is right there. She can do it herself."

"Not without looking desperate."

Dee nodded. "Yeah, I see your point. You're a really good friend."

"I try." Sam beamed in Anna's direction as she and

Monty approached with the luggage cart full of food. "Glad you could make it."

"Me too," Anna said, squinting into the sun. She pulled her sunglasses out of her purse and put them on. It was a gloriously perfect, no-smog day; the sun reflecting off the sandy beach was blinding, the Santa Monica Mountains were visible in the distance.

Anna helped the group set the food out on the long buffet table. She hadn't been down to funky Venice Beach in years, but the carnival atmosphere hadn't changed as far as she could see. Ocean Front Walk, which ran parallel to the beach, was still lined with an eclectic variety of street performers and vendors pushing their wares. People of all ages zigged and zagged on skates or skateboards along the bike path. Tourists strolled along, taking photos of the local color.

A crowd began to gather around the buffet table, shouting questions at them. Who were they, how much was the food, who was the food for?

"For everyone," Sam replied. "People!" she yelled to the growing crowd. "This food is free for all those who are hungry. Please form a line starting right here."

"But only if you're, like, poor and homeless and stuff," Dee added. "We just want to do good deeds."

Cammie checked her watch. "Where the hell is Parker?"

"He probably stopped to have new publicity shots taken," Sam cracked.

"He's got my Mercedes," Cammie snapped. "If he stops anyplace besides Breckner's, he's dead."

"Hey, when do we start eating?" someone in the crowd yelled.

"You've got a five-thousand-dollar Nikon around your neck!" Sam yelled back. "Get out of the line, bozo!"

"The natives are way restless," Dee muttered.

Anna looked over the line as it snaked down the board-walk. There was a toothless man so filthy it was impossi-ble to discern the color of his shirt, who wore a weathered cardboard sign around his neck that read, THE WORLD'S GREATEST WINO. Right behind were some upscale yuppies in designer beachwear eager for a free meal. A couple who looked to be in their sixties, com-pletely covered in tattoos, held hands, waiting patiently.

"People, welcome to Venice!" a man on inline skates, guitar in hand, called out to the crowd. His dreadlocks were piled into a turban, and he wore purple harem pants. "I'm Ace Pace, world's most famous street performer! I'm here to make your day!" He skated around the board-walk in large circle formations and played old Beatles songs on his electric guitar, his amp strapped to his arm.

"I think he was in *White Men Can't Jump!*" one of the tourists exclaimed, and everyone began snapping Ace's photo.

This was all very entertaining, but Anna was desper-ate for about four more hours of sleep, and she wasn't clear on what the program was supposed to be. "What are we waiting for, exactly?" she asked Sam.

"We're waiting for Mrs. Breckner, our project adviser."

Anna was confused. "Sorry?"

"At Beverly Hills High, you have to do community service first semester every year. The report has to be turned in by the first day back after winter vacation, which is day after tomorrow."

The truth was slowly beginning to dawn on Anna. "So this was the last day you—all of you—could do it."

Sam nibbled on a stalk of marinated asparagus. "Can I help it if we have busy social lives? Parker went to pick up Breckner in Van Nuys like an hour ago. She has to be here before we start to sign off on it."

Anna felt slightly ill. "You feed the homeless every New Year's Day for school credit. Because it's the last chance you've got to do it."

Sam shrugged. "If you want to get technical about it."

"So why the hell did you invite me?"

Sam looked wounded. "Excuse me for including you!"

"You weren't exactly honest with me."

Sam put one hand on her hip and gave Anna a jaded look. "I told you we were feeding the homeless, and we are. I'm sorry if my motives aren't *pure* enough for you."

Anna just shook her head. It was like she and Sam weren't even speaking the same language. "I'm going for a walk," she announced to Sam, interrupting her own thoughts. "I've got a phone call to make."

Without waiting for Sam's response, Anna took off down the boardwalk. When she was far enough away so that Ace's rendition of "Hey Jude" was only a distant refrain, she pulled out her cell phone. She had to make contact with someone real. Someone she cared about, who cared about her.

For a moment, though, she was struck by the glory of a perfect Los Angeles afternoon. The sky was a crystal-clear aquamarine, the temperature midsixties. Anna could smell the sand and the surf, almost taste the ocean salt on her tongue. The only visible pollution was that of the human variety.

At that moment Anna wished—so much!—that her sister were there with her. She took out her phone and pressed in a speed-dial number.

"Hazelden," answered a disembodied voice. "May I help you?"

"Good morning. May I speak to Susan Percy, please?"

"Please hold. I'll see if she's available."

Anna waited. And waited. Then she heard a tentative voice.

"Hello?"

"Susan? It's Anna! Happy New Year!"

"Anna."

There was silence after that. Had they changed her sister's meds? Was she mad at her? What?

"Sooz? You there?"

"Yeah. It's just . . . well, congratulations on being the only member of our family who's bothered to call me."

So Susan wasn't mad. She was hurt. God, how had their family gotten so screwed up? "They'll call, Sooz," Anna insisted, though she knew it wasn't true.

"Bullshit. Mom is in Italy recuperating from the trauma of being our mother. And Dad never calls."

Anna didn't know what to say. "So, how are you?"

"Shitty."

"It takes a while," Anna reminded her.

"Please don't start with the clichés."

"But it's true."

"Goody. Something to look forward to."

Anna decided to change the subject. "So, guess where I am?"

"Kansas?"

Anna laughed. "I'm in Los Angeles."

"Good Lord, why?"

"I decided to spend some time here. With Dad."

"And I repeat: Good Lord, why?"

"Lots of reasons. I don't want to talk about me. I want to talk about—"

"Me. But there's nothing to say, Anna. This place sucks. I stuff candy in my face and suck down cigarettes so I won't crawl out of my skin. Meanwhile, my skin feels like it wants to crawl off of me."

"Maybe when you get out, you can come out to L.A. and we can spend some time together," Anna ventured.

"Maybe. But if I do, I'm not staying with Dad. I'll stay at a hotel."

"Okay. Whatever you want."

"Maybe I'll come soon."

Anna didn't like the way that sounded. "What do you mean?" she asked cautiously.

"I'm thinking of checking myself out."

"Susan, you can't do that."

"Don't tell me what the hell I can do!"

Anna winced. "I meant, you shouldn't."

"You don't know what it's like here." Susan's voice dropped to a conspiratorial tone. "This place could drive anyone to drink."

"We'll find you another place, then."

"I don't *want* another place. I want my life back."

Anna grasped the phone so hard that her knuckles turned white. "You just think that because you haven't had a drink or any drugs in a while and—"

"No shit, Sherlock."

"I just meant—"

"I know exactly what you meant." Susan's voice was softer now. "I don't mean to take my shit out on you, Anna. Ignore me. I suck."

"I just . . . I want what's best for you."

"Maybe what's best for me is some time with my baby sister in La La Land. The sharks out there will eat you alive, little sister."

"I'm not so little anymore," Anna reminded her. "I can take care of myself. Susan, if you'd just stay until you finish the program and then—"

"You don't want me to come?"

"Of course I want you to come. It's just—"

"Yadda, yadda, yadda. I know you mean well, Anna. But you can't live my life for me. If I screw this up, it's going to be my screwup. That's just the way it is."

Anna exhaled deeply. "Okay."

"That's my girl. So I'll talk to you soon, 'kay?"

"All right. I love you, Sooz."

"Me too, baby sis. Bye."

"Bye." Anna disconnected the call and put her phone away.

Was Susan really going to check herself out and come to Los Angeles? It would be wonderful to have an ally out here, and when Susan was sober, she was always Anna's ally. But the question would always be, how long would she stay sober? How soon would Anna have to pick up the pieces? Well, whatever else her father insisted on dredging up when she saw him later, they were going to talk about Susan. And he was damn well going to call his older daughter and wish her a happy New Year.

Twenty-three

"Anna?"

Parker Pinelli was heading down the board-walk toward her. "Hey. I thought I saw you. How's it going?"

Once again Anna noted Parker's resemblance to James Dean, circa *East of Eden*. She'd first rented this movie on Cynthia's insistence, having read the John Steinbeck novel on her own when she was in ninth grade. Something about the painful parent-child relationships in it—the grown child whose ceaseless efforts to win the parents' love bear no fruit—made her think of her sister, Susan. Again.

"Parker Pinelli. From the wedding?"

"Right, I remember. Hi."

"So, you hitched a ride with my brother, huh?"

"Sorry?"

"Monty? He told me he picked you up. He's my brother."

"Right, he said that. Sorry, I'm not firing on all cylinders yet."

"No prob," Parker said good-naturedly. "Pretty wild last night, huh? You missed a great night at Sam's—we split from that Warners thing and went to her house. You and Ben should have hung out. So, what'd you guys do?"

Anna's stomach gurgled. She was beginning to feel kind of queasy. She couldn't tell if it was from exhaustion, the phone call with her sister, or the mention of Ben's name. Probably all of the above, she concluded.

"Oh, you know," she said vaguely, wanting to change the subject. "Aren't you supposed to be feeding the homeless for school credit?"

"Nah, I just came to hang with my friends. I finished my community service weeks ago. I volunteer at the Actors Home. There are all these old movie stars there, you know, like from the thirties and forties? They tell these amazing Hollywood stories. It's great."

Anna was touched. "It's nice you do that."

"Hey, you gotta find connections where you can." He raised his face to the sun. "It's nice out, huh? We used to live in Chicago. The weather there sucked. So, want to take a walk?"

Why not? Anna had no particular desire to join the others. They began to stroll in the opposite direction, past incense stands, henna artists, and blankets covered with bad paintings for sale. Silver jewelry stands gave way to a young man selling a hand-size airplane that followed his verbal commands. There was a crowd around a guy in shorts who kept up comic banter while balancing a girl in a chair on his chin. Farther down, a street performer blew fire at an impressed crowd, who dropped coins and bills in the top hat in front of him.

"It's wild down here, huh?" Parker asked.

"I kind of like it," Anna said. "I could see living down here."

"Careful," Parker teased, "they'll take away your membership at the Beverly Hills Country Club for saying something like that."

"To tell you the truth, I'm not all that crazy about Beverly Hills."

"Come on," Parker chided. "*Everyone* wants to live in Beverly Hills."

They passed a stand that boasted "the largest selection of sunglasses on the planet," and, beyond that, a woman with graying hair down to her knees who gave neck and back massages. Her sign promised twenty minutes of heaven for twenty dollars.

"Hey, Monkey Man!" Parker called, waving to an elderly man with a small monkey perched on his shoulder.

"How ya doin', Parker?" the man called back.

"Come on, I'll introduce you," Parker said, and they hustled over. "We were both extras in a film together last year. This guy's the best."

"Parker, Lulu's been askin' aboutcha," Monkey Man said, flashing a nearly toothless smile.

"Aw, Lulu, I missed you, too," Parker said, giving the monkey a kiss. She screeched happily, hopping around on Monkey Man's shoulder, and kissed Parker back. He introduced Anna to Monkey Man.

"Lulu's got a crush on your boyfriend," he told Anna.

"He's not my boyfriend," Anna said, laughing as Lulu jumped into Parker's arms and covered him with monkey kisses. "But if he were, I'd be proud to lose him to a girl like Lulu."

Monkey Man pointed a long finger at Anna. "I like this girl."

When Lulu finally allowed herself to be torn from Parker's arms, he and Anna headed farther down the boardwalk. Two boys walked by eating chili dogs, and the scent wafted over to Anna. Her stomach turned. Maybe she was getting sick.

"Parker, would you mind if we headed back?"

"No prob." He peered at her. "Are you okay? You got kind of pale all of a sudden."

"Probably just my New York pallor," Anna joked, but she was suddenly freezing. They turned back and Anna rubbed her arms to warm up.

Parker slipped off his leather jacket. "Here, wear this."

"No, that's okay—"

But he'd already settled his jacket around Anna's shoulders, a gesture that reminded her of Ben. Why did every damn thing remind her of Ben?

"You and Ben partied a little too hard last night, huh?" Parker guessed, almost as if he were reading her mind. She made a deliberate decision to banish Ben from her thoughts. Ben Birnbaum is nothing to me, she told herself. Less than nothing.

"So, you're an actor, right?" Anna coaxed, just to fill her mind with something other than Him.

"Yeah, I'm up for a guest-starring role for this mid-season replacement. My agent says it's down to me and one other guy."

"When will you hear?"

"He said something about after the Jewish holiday."

Anna tried to think what Jewish holiday he could possibly be talking about. Hanukkah ended before Christmas; that much she knew. Passover wasn't until the spring. Nothing else came to mind.

Anna's stomach gurgled again. Even with Parker's leather jacket on, she was shivering. "You really don't look so hot," Parker told her.

"I'm okay," Anna insisted, though she wasn't certain it was true. But she wasn't about to make a scene just because she was cold and her stomach was a little upset.

Parker slowed down and scratched the perfect cleft in his chin. "Listen, Anna, before we get back with the others, there's something I wanted to say to you."

"What?"

"I hope you don't think this is out of line. I mean, I know you don't know me and I don't know you, but you seem like a really cool girl."

"Whatever you want to say, just say it," Anna told him.

"Yeah. Well, it's about Birnbaum," Parker said. "You just met the guy, right?"

"Right."

"He comes on like he's all that. But there are some

things you don't know about him that you probably sh—"

"Hey, you two, come help!" Sam called to them.

The line was even longer than it had been before. Parker held up a finger, as in "one minute."

"Go on," Anna urged him, her voice low. "What about Ben?"

"Yo, big bro, throw out some of this trash for us," Monty asked, waving a giant plastic trash bag in Parker's direction.

"Be right there."

Anna reached for Parker's arm. "Parker . . ."

"We can talk later," Parker said.

Anna told herself to drop it. Hearing more about Ben, good or bad, was like aluminum foil pressing on a dental filling. But she couldn't help herself. "You'll tell me later?"

Parker mumbled something unintelligible, then scratched behind one ear and ambled over to the table to grab the garbage bag from his brother. As far as Anna was concerned, his refusal to make eye contract with her was the body language of a man who was having second thoughts.

Twenty-four

"Hot coffee, hot coffee, coming through," Monty bellowed. He offered his cardboard box full of to-go coffees to everyone behind the table. "Sam?"

"Thanks, Monty."

"I live to serve," he said cheerfully, offering the coffee box to Mrs. Breckner. "Very sweet of you," she said. The teacher grabbed a cup and two sugars.

"Hey, it's New Year's Day; I figured everyone could use it. So what'd you do last night for New Year's Eve, Mrs. Breckner?"

"Not much. A small voodoo ceremony with close friends," she deadpanned, sipping her coffee.

Sam chuckled. She liked Mrs. Breckner, who, frankly, was the best English teacher she'd ever had. Sam could almost see a *To Sir, with Love* thing going on if Sidney Poitier had been white, Jewish, and dumpy, clad in a deeply awful peach pantsuit.

"Dee?" Monty held out the coffee box.

"No thanks. Coffee is very bad for you, Monty. It's processed with known carcinogens. It can give you can-

198

cer and make you grow extra toes."

Sam gawked at Dee. "Where do you get these things?"

"*Organic Living Today* magazine. I'll pick one up for you next time I'm at Whole Foods." Dee placed a scoop of caviar onto a paper plate and passed it to the wild-eyed woman in rags who stood before her, then craned around to their teacher. "We've served three hundred meals, Mrs. Breckner," Dee called. "How many more do we have to do?"

"There's still plenty of food left and plenty of people," Mrs. Breckner said. "Knock yourself out and hang in there for a while, Delia. Think of all the points you'll get in heaven. You too, Sam."

"God doesn't keep a scorecard, Mrs. Breckner," Dee said solemnly.

"Can we just finish, Dee, without you picking a fight with her?" Sam hissed to Dee. "I need her recommendation to get into Princeton."

Dee stopped serving and turned to Sam. "What do you mean, Princeton? Since when are you going to Princeton?"

"I didn't say I'm going; I said I'm applying."

"You've got like a 4.3 average, Sam. You'll get in."

"Not necessarily."

"And you did 800 on your verbal SATs."

"And 650 on math," Sam reminded her. "Other negatives: I'm rich. I'm white."

Dee shifted her weight and blocked the sun with her hands so she could see Sam better. "So why do you want to go there?"

"Last I heard, it was a really good school."

Dee knew that. But what if Sam wanted to go to Princeton because Ben went to Princeton? Or was she just being Little Miss Paranoid? Her eyes slid over to Anna and Parker, who'd just rejoined them. Anna was wearing Parker's jacket. Dee nudged Sam. "Unbelievable."

"What?"

"Anna. Look at her. She was with Ben last night and she had his jacket, too. That innocent act is such a crock."

"She had Ben's jacket because Cammie ripped her dress off," Sam reminded Dee.

"It was an accident. Right, Cammie?"

"Would I do something that nasty?" Cammie asked, bringing another stack of paper plates over to Sam and Dee.

Dee let that one slide. "So, how late did you stay at the party last night?"

Cammie shrugged. "Who knows?"

"You should have come to Sam's. We went skinny dipping."

"Big whup."

"Shut up. It was fun."

Cammie almost smiled. "Who'd you end up with, Delia?"

"Oh, you know . . . ," Dee said evasively.

"Parker," Sam filled in.

"We made out in the pool, that's all." Her eyes cut to Parker and Anna again. "That Anna is like a man-eater or something!"

"Literally," Cammie said smugly. "She must be very talented, considering Ben's reaction. And now she's your new friend, Sam. I could weep."

"I only invited her to pump her about her date with Ben on your behalf," Sam protested.

Cammie pushed some strawberry-and-gold curls off her face. "Or maybe you're hoping some of her East Coast WASPy perfection will rub off on you."

Heat came to Sam's cheeks. Sometimes Cammie scared the hell out of her; it was like she was inside Sam's head. "That's ridiculous."

"I know," Cammie agreed. "But it's also true."

"Hey, guys, do we have any seltzer or anything like that?" Parker asked, coming over to the girls. "Anna's stomach is kind of upset."

"Gee, don't say hi, Parker," Dee said pointedly.

He looked at her blankly. "I said hi to you before, Dee. Get any sleep?"

"You know I didn't," Dee replied. "And I know *you* didn't."

"My bad," Parker said, pointing at himself cheerfully. "Last night was fun, huh? So, we got seltzer for Anna?"

"Go buy her some if it means that much to you," Dee suggested through clenched teeth.

He looked at her curiously. "You pissed about something, Dee?"

"No."

"Yeah, you are." He came around the table and

tipped Dee's face up to his. "Hey, you upset? Because I care about how you feel."

"No, you don't."

"Wow." Parker put his hands to his heart. "You misjudge me, Dee. We'll talk later, okay?" He headed off to find seltzer.

"That boy is such a player," Sam said.

"You realize he doesn't give a rat's ass about you, Delia, right?" Cammie asked.

"So? I'm not into him, either. But he had his tongue down my throat last night. I don't appreciate being ignored."

"Good for you, Dee," Sam cheered. "Stick up for yourself!"

"Well, I'm not jealous, anyway. Parker and I fooled around, that's all. There's another guy I like."

"Really?" Sam asked. "Who?"

Dee looked away. "Just someone."

Fifty feet away, Anna felt her stomach churn dangerously. She took off Parker's jacket, since she'd gone from freezing to a cold sweat in about thirty seconds. Something was definitely wrong with her. She walked behind the buffet table. "Is there a glass of water I could have?"

"All we've got is orange juice and it's probably warm by now," Sam said, noting that Anna really did look a little sick. "Parker went to get you seltzer. You want the juice?"

The thought of warm orange juice almost made Anna gag. "No. Thanks."

Mrs. Breckner frowned at Anna. "You're not one of

my students."

"She's a friend of mine who just moved here from New York," Sam explained, introducing Anna to the teacher.

"Will we be seeing you at Beverly Hills High?" Mrs. Breckner asked.

"No. I'll be doing an internship at Randall Prescott." *I hope,* she added mentally. Suddenly Anna's legs felt rubbery. *I hope.* She really needed to sit down. But there was nowhere to sit other than some stone benches quite a ways down the boardwalk.

"So Anna, how was the rest of the evening with Ben?" Dee asked. "We missed you at Sam's!"

Anna's face betrayed nothing. "Fine."

"Dee," Sam chided. "That's really none of our business."

"But you said you invited her to—"

Sam shot Dee a warning look. It took Dee a beat to catch on. "Oh. You're right," Dee admitted. "Whatever you and Ben did last night is your business. That was a real invasion of your personal space, Anna. Sorry."

"Not a problem," Anna said graciously, feeling worse by the minute. Sweat beaded up on her forehead. Maybe Ben had given her the flu.

"So when are you and Ben going out again?" Sam asked brightly.

"I thought you just said—," Dee began.

"I'm asking as a friend, not prying," Sam explained. "There's a difference."

Ben again. When would it end? Anna wished she

could just banish him from the planet.

"I don't really know," Anna replied.

"He's such a great guy," Dee said in her little girl voice, sighing.

Anna felt like yelling, No! He's not! He's an asshole and a player and I fell for his line of shit.

"Hickey alert," Cammie said, pointing at Dee's neck. "I didn't notice it before. How funny. And just where did you leave your mark on Parker last night, Delia?"

Parker and Dee? Anna wondered. But at the wedding, hadn't Parker been with that girl Skye? These people were like sexual pickup sticks: Throw them in the air and they land in a whole new configuration.

"Thank God, no more chicken," Sam said, shoveling the last piece onto a paper plate. "Monty!" she yelled. "We need more garbage bags!"

"Seltzer," Parker pronounced, trotting over with a cold plastic cup and handing it to Anna. "At your service."

"Thanks." Anna sipped it. It didn't seem to help. Her stomach felt queasy again, worse than before. She concentrated on deep breathing and willed the feeling away.

Sam peered at Anna more closely. "Seriously. You look like shit."

"I'm not feeling very well, actually," Anna admitted. "I really think I need to leave. I wonder if Monty could—"

"Say cheese, everyone!" Monty ordered as he aimed a camera at the group. "Move in closer. This one's for the yearbook!"

Before Anna could protest that she shouldn't be in

the photo because she, thank God, didn't go to their school, and before she could say again how truly, deeply awful she felt, the group was pressing in on her: Sam on one side and Cammie on the other, one big, happy group of really keen friends.

"Please, I have to—," Anna groaned, but everyone was talking and mugging for the camera. Monty begged for one more shot. Cammie "playfully" leaned in, blocking Anna from the shot.

"Cammie!"

Something about the distress in Anna's voice made Cammie turn toward her. Anna opened her mouth again to explain that she felt like she was going to be sick. But before she could say it, she *was* it and puked all over Cammie.

Just as Monty snapped the photo.

Vomit dripped from Cammie's red curls onto her lemon-yellow silk Marc Jacobs camisole. It oozed down her gold Calvin Klein leather jacket and landed on the toes of her fawn-colored Gucci suede boots. Cammie cursed hysterically.

Anna would have been terribly humiliated, except that she passed out and missed the whole thing.

Twenty-five

Anna groaned. Her throat was on fire and her stomach muscles ached. She forced herself to open her eyes, but the bright sunlight streaming in through the picture window of her bedroom was so painful that she quickly shut them again.

So. At least she knew where she was: at her father's house, in her own bed. She remembered getting dog sick in Venice. She remembered coming to in the back of the SUV. She remembered Sam sitting next to her, filing her nails and explaining that she had volunteered to stay with Anna, not to be nice, but so she could get out of cleaning up.

When Anna had opened her mouth to thank Sam, she'd puked all over again. And that was pretty much the last thing she remembered.

Anna opened her eyes and managed to keep them open. She struggled to a sitting position but felt so weak that she slumped back against the pillows.

"Here, let me help you," came a baby wisp of a voice.

Dee? Dee was in the room with her? *Dee,* of all people?

Yes, Dee. She rushed over from the chaise longue to help ease Anna up. Then she gently plumped the pillows behind her head.

"Thanks," Anna croaked.

"Take it easy," Dee counseled as she gave her a bottle of Gatorade. "Drink this for the electrolytes. Baby sips, or you might hurl again."

"Thank you." Anna took a few sips and then cleared her throat. "Very much."

"Well, that sounds a little better." Dee sat on the edge of Anna's bed. "How crappy do you feel?"

"Extremely. How did I get home?" Anna put a hand on her stomach. It was bare. "And undressed?"

"Oh, we helped you."

"We?"

"Me and Sam. Cammie was covered with puke, so she had to go home. You even got her hair," Dee added cheerfully. "Nice shot."

Anna closed her eyes again. Oh God. *That* she remembered.

"Not that Cammie would've helped you, anyway," Dee added. "What with you stealing her boyfriend and everything."

There was a soft knock on the door; Anna's father stuck his head inside. "Oh, good. You're awake!"

"Sort of," Anna said.

"How do you feel?"

"Awful. But not *as* awful."

"You had a mean case of food poisoning," her father explained.

"From what? All I ate was a yogurt from your refrigerator."

"We found the container in the SUV," Dee explained. "The expiration date was in November."

Jonathan winced. "My housekeeper two housekeepers ago lived on that stuff. I fired her around Halloween."

"But it tasted fine," Anna protested.

Dee nodded. "That's lemon yogurt for you. It's tart whether it's good *or* bad."

Anna's father grinned at Dee. "Good thing Anna made such a great friend so quickly."

"Well, she's pretty special," Dee said.

Anna's head reeled. Maybe she was dreaming. Dee was sitting at her bedside, telling her father how special she was.

"Think you can handle tea, Anna?" her father asked. "And maybe some dry toast?"

Anna was touched. "That would be great, Dad. Thanks."

"Margaret told me to ask you. I'll go tell her. Be back soon." Her father closed the door behind him as he departed.

Margaret. Tea and toast hadn't even been her father's idea. Swell.

Dee stood up and stretched, exposing her navel ring. "Wow. Your father's hot. How old is he?"

"Could we discuss my father later? Can you please fill me in on what happened?"

"Oh, sure. You know, you ought to think about bringing in a feng shui consultant for this room."

"Dee—"

"All right. It's just bad energy to have your bed facing north like that."

Dee's mangled Eastern philosophy was making Anna queasy all over again. "Dee, could you please just stick to the story?"

"Oh, okay, sure. Well, you puked again in the back of the SUV. Do you remember that part? Sam's jeans are history. I had some yoga pants in the back of my car, so she changed into those. But they're an extra small, so they were really, really tight on her, which wasn't very attractive, and I felt so bad for her, you know? I would have brought some in a large if I had known—"

"Dee." Anna's head was pounding. "Can you maybe give me the short version?"

"Oh yeah. Out here it's called coverage. Anyway, Mrs. Breckner called her family doctor and he said you wouldn't die from eating bad yogurt, so we could just take you home. So we did."

"Define 'we' one more time."

"Monty, Sam, and me," Dee recited. "You don't remember that part?"

"Some of it. I kept falling asleep and waking up and—"

"Wow." Dee's eyes got enormous. "You mean you don't remember the stuff you said?"

Anna shook her head.

"You were mumbling something about fucking Ben."

Anna threw a hand over her eyes. "I didn't."

"I wouldn't make something like that up."

Anna had zero recollection of saying *anything* about Ben, much less about having sex with him. Which she hadn't. Maybe she'd been using *fucking* as an adjective. Fucking Ben. Like that.

"Anyway, what happened with you and Ben last night?"

"Look, Dee, I appreciate that you helped me when I was sick. And I appreciate that you stayed with me—"

"Oh, well. I'm a nice person. Even if you don't really like someone, it's too mean to just, like, leave them." Dee sat on the edge of Anna's bed. "But you were just about to tell me what happened with you and Ben last night. Did you do him?"

"That's not really any of your business, Dee."

"Yeah, actually it is. You think you know Ben, but you don't."

"Believe me, Dee. I have no illusions that I know him."

"But you know where he is."

Anna's heart skipped a beat. "What do you mean?"

"I mean, I called him this morning, and his mom said he never came home last night. So where is he?"

Anna exhaled slowly. "I don't know, Dee." The pain and humiliation of last night came rushing back. Anna sipped her Gatorade defensively.

Dee stood up and put her hands on her hips. "What is it with you people? It's because I'm short, isn't it?"

Anna shook her head. "Sorry, what?"

"No one takes me seriously. Not Cammie, not Sam, not you."

"Dee, I—"

"Just because a person is spiritual and short doesn't make her stupid, okay? Ben told you not to tell me where he is, right?"

What? "No, of course not."

"Bullshit." Dee got up and paced Anna's gleaming hardwood floor. "Yes. That's exactly what happened. You're covering for him."

"Dee, I have no idea what you're—"

"I know you don't. No one does. Except Ben." Dee looked almost smug. "And you thought it was Cammie you had to worry about. I *let* you think that. I let *everyone* think that." She stood at the foot of Anna's bed and blew her wispy bangs off her forehead. "It's like this. Six weeks ago Ben and I hooked up at Princeton."

Anna tried to wrap her mind around this piece of news. "You did?"

"I was on a college tour with my parents. I'm not going to Princeton, but there's this really good junior college near there. So anyway, I called Ben. Just a friendly phone call, you know? So he invited me for a drink. So I went." She dropped her hands from her diminutive hips. "And we ended up having a lot more than a drink."

Anna was starting to feel queasy again. "Could you please just tell me whatever it is you're trying to tell me, Dee?"

"Sure. It's pretty simple. I'm pregnant. And it's Ben's baby."

Twenty-six

3:54 P.M., PST

A nna slipped her feet into velvet flip-flops. She felt
marginally better—physically, at least. She'd managed to doze for a while after Dee departed. But the late
afternoon sun slashed wedges of ochre light through
the window and across her face, awakening her.

Now she sat on the edge of her bed, feeling empty.
What bizarre confluence of cosmic events had dropped
her in the midst of this Beverly Hills teen psychodrama,
starring Ben, Sam, Cammie, and Dee? Had Dee even
told her the truth? Had anyone?

It was too much to handle alone. Yet she couldn't
call her mother in Italy and cry long-distance on her
shoulder; not only was it past midnight in Venice, but
they never shared that kind of intimacy. Her sister,
Susan, had her own problems. Her father? Suffice to
say that the promised tea and toast had never showed
up. The only person in the world with whom she even
came close to having that kind of relationship was Cyn.
And even so, in the *This Is How We Do Things* Big
Book, sobbing about one's own misfortunes was on the

page-one list of Things Not Done in Public (with *public* defined as "the actual or virtual presence of anyone other than oneself").

Well, too bad. Anna had Cyn on speed dial. After three rings . . .

"Yeah?"

"Cyn? It's me."

"Anna! I was just thinking about you, you bitch!"

Was Cyn mad at her, too? "What's wrong?"

"You're not here, that's what's wrong. Do you have any idea how much I miss you?"

That was just so Cyn. Anna got off her bed and curled up on the chaise by the window. Outside, she could see the year's first sunset paint the western sky orange, bloodred, and purple, like a canvas by Seurat.

"I miss you more. How's New York?"

"Cold. But I'm guessing you didn't call to talk about the weather. . . . So, is he?"

"Is who what?"

"The guy from the plane—I forgot his name."

Anna's heart clenched. "Ben. His name is Ben Birnbaum."

"Yeah. Did he turn out to be the man of your dreams?"

Hardly.

"Anna? You still there?"

Anna blinked. "Yes, sorry."

"So? Ben?" Cyn prompted.

"Oh, Cyn, he—"

"Hey, Cyn! Come get 'em while they're hot!"

Anna's heart sank as she recognized the distant male voice calling to her friend.

"Be right there!" Cynthia shouted back. "Hey, Anna?"

"Yes?"

"Guess who's here, cooking me pancakes even as we speak?"

Anna already knew. "Scott?"

"Oh my God, Anna, I had the best time last night. And this morning. And this afternoon. I'm so happy!"

Anna mustered up all the warmth in her voice that she possibly could. "That's fantastic."

"You know those other times with those other guys that I don't count?" Cynthia went on. "Well, now I know why. This was what I always dreamed of."

"I'm so happy for you." Anna was careful not to let her voice betray any of her own pain.

"I'm happy for me, too. So, you were just about to tell me about Ben."

"Oh, it can wait." Anna couldn't bring herself to share her troubles with Cyn. Much as she wanted to, this was Cyn's moment—she loved her friend too much to rain on her parade.

"No, seriously, I want to hear all about—hold on." Anna heard Cyn put her palm over the phone. A moment later she was back. "Anna, he's, like, *summoning* me. He made me chocolate chip pancakes. Isn't that sweet?"

"Very," Anna agreed. "Go eat them. We can talk tomorrow."

"You sure?"

"Absolutely."

"Okay, then. Hey, I was thinking, Scott and I should come out and visit. You and Ben and me and Scott—we'd have a blast, huh?"

"Sure," Anna managed.

"Oh, Anna." Cyn sighed. "I hate it that you're not here. You're my homegirl and you always will be, even if you are out there in that unnatural year-round warm weather sunshine shit. So we'll talk tomorrow and I'll see you soon, right?"

"Absolutely."

They said their good-byes and hung up.

Anna just sat there. She understood that she led a privileged life; she wasn't one to snivel over the vagaries of her own existence. But a veritable bell jar of despair was settling over her. What had she done to deserve this? Had she wanted to forget Scott so badly, been so desperate to love someone who might love her back, that she'd been blind, deaf, and incredibly dumb about everything? It was as if she had invented Ben, spun him out of her own neediness into what it was she wanted him to be. What could she have been thinking?

She gazed at the waning sunset and saw her ravaged face reflected in the window glass. Look what this place was doing to her. She tried to make a mental list of good reasons *not* to return to Manhattan.

But she couldn't even think of one.

She sat heavily on her bed. There was no reason to stay here.

"Anna?" Followed by a soft knock on her door. "May I come in?"

"Yes."

Her father entered, carrying a tray. "I brought toast and tea up to you before, but you'd fallen asleep and I didn't want to wake you. I made some broth, if you think you can keep it down."

"Don't you mean *Margaret* made it?"

"No, I did. She left a while ago. Do you want to try it?"

Anna shook her head.

He took in her desolation. "Do you want to talk about why you're so upset?"

Anna didn't want to even think about all the reasons, there were so many. So she went for the one most directly related to him. "Let's start with the note you left me. About my internship?"

"I'm still hoping to work it out . . ."

"Work *what* out?"

"Margaret's an agent at Randall Prescott. You were going to be her intern—"

"You've got to be kidding me. You were going to have me intern with your girlfriend? And when were you planning on sharing that little detail with me?"

"Margaret happens to be a brilliant woman, Anna, and a good friend. Anyway, she had some blowup yesterday with Pierce Randall, and she quit."

"She quit," Anna echoed flatly.

"They've fought before, so maybe they'll work it

out. Pierce is a jerk. He's had a thing for Margaret for years and—"

"Stop!" Anna put her hands over her ears. "I don't care. I'm sorry if that sounds rude, but it's just . . . I can't deal with all that now. What am I supposed to do, go to *school*?"

"I'll make a few phone calls. I'm sure we can get you into Harvard-Westlake. It's the best private school out here. Supposedly it's up to Trinity's standards."

"Ducky. Just ducky."

"I know it's a bummer, Anna."

Anna peered at her father. "A 'bummer'?"

"I mean, I know that you're disappointed."

"I *know* what the word *bummer* means! I just can't believe it came out of your mouth. You . . . you smoke pot and wander around in grubby clothes and talk like some kind of aging hippie. What happened to you?"

Her father's face closed down. "Same guy."

"Where's the big-time financier in the handmade suits from London?"

"I'm that guy, too."

Anna sighed. "I don't know *who* you are. But I don't suppose it matters anymore."

"It matters to me." Her father sat at her desk and swiped at the day's growth of beard on his chin. "You want to try the soup?"

Anna shook her head.

"You mind if I talk, then? A number of things are bothering me; I'd like to get them off my chest."

"Fine." Selfish to the end, Anna thought. "But I'm going back to New York tomorrow. So at least that's one less bother for you."

"You think you're a bother?"

"I know I am, Dad."

"Jonathan," he corrected her.

"You don't want me here. Maybe on some level you *want* to want me here. So you can feel better about yourself or something. I don't know."

"Christ," her father cussed softly.

"I'd call him, too, if I thought he'd intervene. But somehow I don't think the world works that way. So what is it you wanted to tell me?"

He stood, paced a bit, and then, as he looked out the window, he said, "As a father, I suck."

"I hope you're not waiting for me to disagree with you."

He turned to her. "No, I'm not. I was a crappy father when your mother and I were still married, and I've been an even crappier father since. I'm not proud of that."

Anna crossed her legs smoothly. "So?"

He scratched his chin. "You're not going to make this any easier, I see."

"Was I supposed to?"

"Look, I'm not perfect, okay?"

With a well-bred-young-lady look of faux concern on her face, Anna waited a moment to see if he had more to say. It seemed he didn't. "So that's it, then? That's what you wanted to tell me?"

"I know that act you're putting on, Anna. That polite thing women in this family do on the outside when they're judging you on the inside. I lived with it for years until I couldn't live with it anymore."

"I see. So it's Mom's fault that you sucked as a husband and father. Well, it's all so much clearer to me now."

"I'm trying to tell you something, if you'll climb off that high horse of yours long enough to really listen." Her father sighed. "When I saw you in the gazebo yesterday, it forced me to face some shit that I really did not want to face. I mean, look at you. You're all grown up. And I have no clue how to be a real father to you. So I was an asshole and I made excuses not to meet you and I got stoned and . . . well, like I said, I was an asshole."

"Past *and* present tense," Anna said, her voice brittle.

"There's a point here, Anna. I would like to change."

"Okay. Well, good luck with that, *Jonathan*." She picked up the phone on the nightstand. "Excuse me, please, I'm going to book a flight home."

"Anna, stop. Would you just stop?"

She put the phone down and folded her hands, polite as ever.

"You are so damn much like your mother—"

Anna's temper flared. "You know what? I don't care if I sound like her or act like her, and I don't care if you don't like it. What is it that you want from me? You want me to say I forgive you for being a terrible father? Well, I don't. And neither does Susan. She doesn't even want to be in the same house with you!"

"So she told me on the phone."

Anna was taken aback. "When?"

"Just before I brought your soup upstairs. I called her. Your sister is very angry."

"I know." Anna's voice softened. "I'm glad you called her, though."

"I told her we'd call her together this weekend."

"I won't be here."

"You don't have to leave."

Anna was silent a moment. "There's really no reason for me to stay."

"Anna. I'm just . . ." He held up his palms, as if what he wanted to say couldn't be contained in words. He tried again. "What makes me really sad, what I realized . . . You and Susan. You're my daughters. And I don't know either one of you."

"No," Anna agreed. "You don't."

"When I think of all the years I wasted . . ."

Fear suddenly gripped Anna. Was he dying? "Is it the headaches? Are you sick?"

He waved off her question. "I feel like this is a chance—maybe a last chance for me, for us, to—"

She understood the unspoken part. To know each other. "You didn't feel the need to really know me for seventeen years. Why now?"

He raised one eyebrow. "Some people take longer to grow up than others. Being with Margaret—"

"I don't want to hear about Margaret!"

"Fine, but you'll like her once you know her. I'm in

therapy, too. Maybe you can come with me sometime."

"To see your therapist? No thank you."

"Dr. Fine has helped me see what an adolescent I've been." He lifted his shoulders. "What can I say, Anna? To make you stay?"

She looked down at the tapestry carpet. Nothing. There was nothing he could say. Where did she belong? Back home in New York? It wasn't like she had a parent there, either.

"Come on, Anna. You've already made friends. Those girls who brought you home—"

"Those girls hate me!"

"Nah," he scoffed.

"Yes. And then there's the boy I went to the wedding with . . ." To Anna's shock, a tear trickled down her cheek.

"What did he do?" her father asked, sounding alarmed.

She brushed the tear away. "It doesn't matter anymore."

"Yes, it does. What did he do?"

She didn't answer.

"Anna. What did he do?"

She stared down at her hands, and that made it a little easier. "I thought he thought I was . . . special," she whispered, "but he was only after one thing. God. I sound like every insipid girl from every insipid teen romance novel ever written." She finally raised her eyes to his. "He dumped me when I wouldn't . . . you know."

To Anna's utter mortification, she began to sob. Her father came over to her and wrapped his arms around her. Anna let her head fall to his shoulder, a place it hadn't been since she was nine years old. He rubbed her back and let her sob. Only when it seemed as if she was all cried out did he speak again.

"I hate the bastard."

"Me too." She reached for a box of tissues by her bedside and blew her nose.

"Look, Anna, there are some asshole guys in this world. Evidently you ran into one of 'em."

"Evidently." She blew her nose again.

"I don't know any other way to say this, Anna. I love you and Susan more than anything in the world. I want to learn how to be a father to you. So what I'm asking is . . . would you please stay? Please."

To Anna's shock, tears had welled up in her father's eyes. She wanted to believe—needed to believe—that he was sincere. In the past ten minutes he'd let her into his life more than her mother had in the past seventeen years. And she had let him into hers.

"Can I tell you something?" Anna's voice sounded small to her own ears.

"Anything."

"I don't want to call you Jonathan."

Her father hugged her again, and she cried again. She thought maybe he was crying, too; she couldn't be sure. It was funny, really. She'd come to Los Angeles because she'd thought it would open her up to new and wonderful adventures. But all it had opened her up to so far was heartache.

She could run back home where it was safe, climb right back inside her wealthy little box. She was sure that most of the people she'd met in the past day and a half would love to see her do just that.

Well, screw them.

So what if Ben had used her and three girls whose lives had briefly collided with hers loathed her? She was not going to allow them to make her life miserable or to force her out of town until she was damn well ready to leave.

This might not be the best of times, but Anna refused to allow these people to make it the worst of times, either. When the many-volumed saga of her life was written, Ben, Sam, Cammie, and Dee would barely merit a footnote. But her father would always be there, written or unwritten, on every page.

She needed him. She'd always need him. And as much as he needed to learn how to be her father, Anna knew she needed to learn how to be his daughter.

Two Days Later . . .

BEVERLY HILLS HIGH WELCOMES YOU.

Anna read the sign on the office bulletin board. The feeling was definitely not mutual. Beverly Hills High was pretty much the last place on earth she wanted to be. But contrary to her father's assurances, it had been too late to get her into Harvard-Westlake. And Margaret was still feuding with the owner of the literary agency. Which was how she had ended up here.

"Anna Percy?"

The commotion in the high school's main office was insane; Anna could barely hear the young woman behind the counter call her name. She snaked through the crowd of students. "Yes, that's me."

"I'm Jasmine Grubman—you can call me Jazz, everyone does. I'm one of Mr. Kwan's administrative assistants. Welcome to Beverly Hills High."

Jasmine, midtwenties, size nothing, with artificial breasts so outsized that Anna was surprised she didn't topple over, handed Anna a schedule of classes and a map of the school.

"You'll find everything you need here. Locker combination, class schedule, et cetera. Your locker is in the Lucas wing, through the courtyard. Your homeroom is in the Asner wing—"

"Hey, Jazz. Happy New Year."

Anna turned. Adam Flood had just walked into the office. He looked comfortable and cute in baggy cords and a blue V-necked sweater over a white T-shirt.

"Happy New Year, Adam," Jazz replied happily.

Adam half bowed to Anna. "And to you, Anna."

"Well, hi," Anna said, finding herself truly glad to see him.

"Hi. You look great."

Sweet of him to say so, but Anna hadn't given it a whole lot of thought when she'd dressed that morning—she never really did when she went to school. Back in New York outsized jeans—preferably from some vintage store—ancient sweats, and stretched-out sweaters with obvious holes were all considered not only appropriate, but hip. The idea was to look as if you didn't give a shit.

This morning Anna had pulled on a pair of jeans and a white thermal T-shirt and topped it off with a camel moth-eaten cashmere cardigan that had definitely seen better days. She'd brushed her hair, tied it back with a clear band, smeared on a little Burt's Bees so her lips wouldn't chap, and called it a day.

But, as she'd quickly learned on her walk from the parking lot to the principal's office, kids at Beverly

Hills High had an entirely different notion of appropriate. Skirts were tiny, sweaters tight, heels high. Girls
who chose jeans wore them low enough to show off
tanned abs, navel rings, belly chains, and/or tattoos.
One girl's lower-back anaconda wriggled as she walked.

"Thanks," Anna told him. "It's nice to see a friendly
face."

Adam nodded. "Right back atcha. Welcome to BHH."

A tall kid with a nose ring muscled between Anna
and the administrator. "Hey, you need to sign this,
Jazz." He thrust a paper at her.

She scanned it quickly. "No, your homeroom
teacher has to sign." She pushed the paper back at him
and he slammed out of the office.

"God, first day back, already I get attitude," Jazz
told Adam.

"So, how's it going?" Adam asked her.

"I did an under-five on *General Hospital* last week,"
Jazz answered with pride.

"Great. So listen, Principal Kwan asked me to show
Anna around."

"Oh, you guys know each other?" Jazz asked.

"Yup. You ready, Anna?"

This was news to Anna. "Sure. That would be great."

"Cool. See you, Jazz. Hang in there—your big
break's right around the corner."

"Yeah, right." A girl in a two-sizes-too-small hot
pink Juicy Couture hoodie snickered as they moved
away.

Adam opened the door for Anna. "So, we meet again."

As they dodged bodies on their way down the crowded corridor, Anna asked, "How did the principal know we know each other?"

"He didn't." Adam pushed open another door that led to an open courtyard and gestured Anna through. "I made that up. The truth is, I was walking by the office and I saw you. Figured you could use a friend. I didn't know you were going to school here."

"I wasn't. It's a long story."

"Anyone else know you're here?"

"You're the first." Anna wished he would also be the last. Because fate had now put her at the same school as Sam, Dee, and Cammie, who were the last three people on the planet she wanted to see. Well, it was a big school. She told herself she could simply be polite and avoid them. It was doable.

"Nice out, huh?" Adam said. "The weather here rocks."

Anna turned her face to the sun. The third of January was glorious: a cloudless sky, sunny, and just cool enough to merit a sweater. There was a major snow-storm back east, which meant that by today, the drifts in Manhattan were already black. Or yellow. Or both.

"When my friends ask me what I like about Los Angeles," Anna began, "first on my list is the weather."

"Mine too. You can ski at Mountain High in the morning and surf at Zuma in the afternoon. We *definitely* didn't have that in Michigan. So, the low-rent tour." Adam opened his arms expansively. "This, obviously, is the BHH grand courtyard. Kids hang out, eat lunch, sneak illegal fill-in-the-blank, like that. Of course, every group hangs on its own turf. "

Anna could easily decode the school pecking order. At a central cluster of picnic tables, beneath a triangle of palm trees, was the school A-list. The girls were the best looking, with the hippest, most expensive clothes and the most attitude. The guys were their Abercrombie male equivalent—hot enough to model for the catalog and rich enough to scoff at the idea of shopping there.

The table closest to the door they'd come through held the geeks—bad skin, hair, bodies—all the money in the world couldn't buy them out of the high school experience from hell. Next to them were the alts. They sat on the ground with their backs against the building, looking disdainful. A handful of goths hung out *under* another picnic table. Meanwhile the flotsam and jetsam of the student silent majority jockeyed for position around the edges of the lawn.

"Maybe we all have microchips in our brains, signaling us to separate into these diverse little groups," Anna mused.

Adam chuckled. "Maybe we do. It wasn't so different in Michigan. The difference is that here, hardly anyone's family has an income under heavy six digits. Come on."

They crossed the courtyard to the two-story Hepburn wing. Adam showed her the state-of-the-art biology and chemistry labs, science library, and class-rooms.

Anna noticed that Adam had buzzed off his hair since the wedding. Now she saw that he had a tiny tat-too behind his left ear, a blue star. He turned and caught her looking at it. And blushed. Which, in Anna's experience, was so *not* Beverly Hills.

He touched his ear self-consciously. "My hair was long when I got it. I refused to cut it for months so my parents wouldn't see the tattoo. My mom hates them."

Anna smiled. She thought it was sweet that his mother would get upset over so tiny a tattoo. Not that she had any body art. Not that she wanted any.

"So, what do you think?" Adam asked.

"I think it's cute."

"I, uh, meant the school. Come on, we can take a shortcut through here." He led her through a side door to an outside passageway. "Now we're heading over to performing arts, also known as the Thank God for Streisand wing."

"Meaning she paid for it?" Anna guessed.

"Hey, she's a Democrat who believes in public edu-cation. So are Michael Douglas, Ed Asner, Spielberg, et cetera, et cetera. They donate all this cool stuff. That way they can send their kids here, feel like they're get-ting the best, and still be politically correct. Believe me, we have everything that kids have at ritzy private schools like Harvard-Westlake. Maybe more. Meanwhile kids down in South Central probably study from science textbooks that say, 'Someday, people hope to put a man on the moon.'"

Adam opened a door and led her into a dark, cool theater. She took in the massive proscenium-arch stage, the orchestra pit, and the endless wing and fly space. "Wow. This must seat a thousand people."

"Pretty awesome, huh?"

"Kids in South Central don't have anything like this, I'm assuming."

"*No one* has anything like this," Adam admitted. "Except us. Hey, I shouldn't bitch about it. It's not like I'm protesting having all the advantages. Like, for example, the gym? Totally state-of-the art." He mimed shooting a foul shot. "The hardwood is the same as in the Staples Center. Our head coach used to coach at Texas Tech, and the sports psychologist for the Lakers works with us. He helped me big time. You like b-ball?"

"Honestly? I don't know much about it."

"Well, if you're ever interested, I'm your man."

Their eyes met. Anna liked what she saw there. "I just might take you up on that. Thanks."

"You're welcome."

Anna's cell phone rang. Who would be calling her on a weekday morning? She wondered if it was Cyn, playing hooky. Or not playing hooky—it wouldn't be the first time Cyn had made a clandestine phone call right under her teacher's nose.

Anna found her phone and checked the incoming call. Her heart skipped a beat. It was Ben.

Now? He was calling her now, just when she was starting to talk herself down? One part of her wanted to tell him just exactly where he could shove his Nokia. Another part of her wanted to demand an explanation for his behavior.

But no. She refused to give in to either of those feelings. She didn't answer but simply dropped her phone back into her purse.

"Ben?" Adam guessed.

"No one important."

"Okay, well, moving on." He checked his watch quickly. "Five minutes until homeroom, and my homeroom teacher is a freak about punctuality."

"Did I make you late?"

"I'm already late—I've got to go back to the main building."

"Well, blame it on the new girl."

"Not a problem." He grinned. "Perks of being a jock with a 4.3 average—"

Anna's phone rang again. She checked the incoming number again. Ben wasn't giving up.

"Aren't you going to answer?" Adam asked.

"Won't some teacher hyperventilate if I used my cell during school?" Anna invented.

Adam nodded. "Where's your homeroom?"

"Uh, let's see." She pulled out her schedule. "Asner 218."

"This way." He walked Anna to an entrance to the courtyard and pointed. "You go straight across to that building. Then up the middle staircase and turn left.

You can't miss it. I don't suppose you're on first lunch, are you?"

"Yes, actually, I think I am."

"Cool. So, I'll look for you. See ya."

"See you. And thanks again."

He loped off, and Anna set off across the courtyard. What a nice guy he was. There was no artifice; what you saw was exactly what you got. It was so refreshing after the many people she'd met in this oh-so-lovely town who reeked of insincerity—

Her cell phone rang for a third time. Ben again. What if he just kept calling and calling? Anna took a deep breath, exhaled, then flipped open her phone.

"Hello?"

"Anna? It's Ben."

Anna felt her knees weaken as she folded into the nearest picnic table. People streamed by, but she didn't see them. Damn Ben, anyway! Why did he have this effect on her?

"Anna? Are you there?"

She found her voice. "I don't want to talk to you." It was a lie. But she desperately wanted it to be the truth.

"Don't hang up," he said quickly. "I have to talk to you."

"Now, two days later, you suddenly expect me to *listen* to you?"

"Please. Anna—"

"No." Sudden fury overcame her. How could she possibly still feel so much desire for such a user, a poser, a . . . a . . .

"Just leave me alone, Ben." She forced herself to disconnect the call and headed into school. The more she thought about Ben, the angrier she got. Anger was good. Anger was strong, stronger than whatever pathetic, needy part of her had fallen for the way he made her feel when his hands were tangled in her hair.

No. Forget him. Concentrate on the here and now. She looked up and froze. *They* were crossing the courtyard toward her. Sam, Cammie, and Dee, suited up in their standard school-day uniforms: designer low-slung pants, formfitting tops, and stiletto-heeled boots.

An absurd image flew into Anna's head: of Cerberus, the monstrous three-headed dog that guarded the gates of Hades, because like Cerberus, all three heads seemed to spot her as one. The six-eyed beast looked surprised to see her.

Anna's heart pounded; her breathing grew shallow. A rivulet of perspiration trickled down her spine. It was one thing to think about ignoring them if—when—she ran into them and quite another for it to actually happen.

"Anna!" Sam called, and led the beast forward. "What are you doing here?"

"There was a last-minute change of plans."

"You're going to school here?" Sam asked.

"For the moment," Anna replied.

"Wow. That's great." Sam touched Anna's arm. "So how are you feeling?"

This was very odd. Sam sounded like she was actually concerned. "Better. Thanks," Anna replied warily.

"Gosh, it's great to see you!" Dee said, actually giving Anna a little hug.

Great to see her? What was *wrong* with these people? The last time Anna had seen Dee, Dee was in her bedroom telling her that she'd hooked up with Ben and that she was *pregnant* with his baby! It was insane!

Anna vowed to keep her composure. She looked over at Cammie. "I apologize if I ruined your clothes when I got sick. I'll replace them."

Cammie's lips smiled, but her eyes remained cold. "Well, there was that little accident with your dress at the wedding. So let's just call it even."

"Fine." Anna cut her eyes at Dee. "And how are *you* feeling, Dee?"

"My tummy has been a little upset," Dee replied, all wide-eyed innocence. She cradled the area below her navel. "Maybe I caught whatever you had."

And maybe you're pregnant, Anna thought. No. That couldn't possibly be true. Could it? Why not? Ben could be having unprotected sex with every girl on the planet—except her—for all Anna knew.

"Well, I'd better get to my homeroom," Anna said. "Nice to see you."

Sam took a few steps backward. "I'll find you later and we'll hang out." She spun around. After a waggle of her tiny fingers in Anna's direction, so did Dee. Anna headed for the Asner wing, her heart still pounding. Suddenly she felt a hand on her shoulder.

"Hold up a minute, Gwynie-poo."

Anna turned. There stood Cammie, by herself.

"I just wanted to add my personal welcome," Cammie said, pulling Anna toward her as if to tell her a secret. "Let me phrase it this way. Watch your back."

Anna's chin jutted out. "Am I supposed to be scared of you?"

"Only if you're smart." Cammie looked around, making sure no one was within hearing distance. "Oh. One last thing. We never had this little conversation." Then, with a final malicious look, she turned and strode off.

Blood rushed to Anna's head. She closed her eyes and breathed deeply, as if an infusion of oxygen could somehow expunge Cammie from her memory. What possible joy could she take in being so evil? Something was seriously wrong with that girl. Why else would she—

"Anna?"

She opened her eyes. Time slowed down and her heartbeat picked up speed. As the person standing before her went into sharp focus, the rest of the world faded. And just as she was beginning to wonder whether she had imagined the events of the last three days, this unexpected visit put her face-to-face with hard evidence to the contrary.

It was Ben.

"Please let me talk to you," Ben said.

She took a step back from him. "How did you even know I was here?"

"I called your father's house and the maid told me you were at school. Please, just give me a chance to explain."

Only now did she notice how terrible he looked: unshaved, wrinkled shirt, bloodshot eyes with dark circles under them. And the son of a bitch was still gorgeous.

Every part of Anna wanted to ask him: How? How could you just leave me like that? Was everything you said to me a lie? Where were you? But she didn't say any of that. She refused to be pathetic. "There's only one thing I want to ask," Anna said, her voice low. "Were you with another girl?"

Ben hesitated. "Yes. But I can explain—"

"Yes, you can." Anna paused as she steeled herself. "To that other girl."

She tried to pass him, but he blocked her way. "I don't blame you for hating me, Anna. I hate myself. Just give me five minutes to explain. After that, if you still hate my guts, I'll never bother you again."

Maybe it was the good breeding instilled by the *This Is How We Do Things* (East Coast edition) Big Book. Or maybe it was the naive, innocent part of her that still believed in Jane Austen, that Elizabeth Bennet would love Mr. Darcy forever. And that Ben was her Mr. Darcy.

A teacher walked by, saw them, and frowned. Anna knew she was supposed to be in her homeroom. "Five minutes," she said. "But not here." She led the way back into the courtyard, keeping as much distance between herself and Ben as possible. "Start talking," she said. "You're on the clock."

He rubbed his bleary eyes. "Okay. Here goes . . ."

Ticktock, Anna thought. He really shouldn't squander his time on the windup.

"One of my really close friends is an actress . . . a name you'd recognize. Actually . . . knowing you . . . you probably have no idea who she is . . . but she's pretty well known."

Did he have to be so damn cute while Anna was trying to hate him? Ben's ribbings about her attention-to-pop-culture-deficit disorder were one of Anna's favorite things about him. And she was deeply touched that in the little time they'd had together, he'd already filed away certain choice factoids about her. But she had to be strong. She had no choice but to resist the adorable side of his personality and focus on the thoughtless, cruel side that left her high and dry.

Ben hesitated, as if he could feel Anna hardening, then continued. "I've known her for a while. We met through my parents."

Was this story going anywhere? "You now have four minutes," Anna said.

"Look, it's not easy to . . ." He stopped, then started again. "This girl's image is squeaky clean. But the truth is, she's an addict—alcohol, pills, you name it. If word got out, she'd be screwed, because the insurance companies for film and TV would refuse to cover her."

"And?" Anna asked coldly.

"So, that night—New Year's Eve—she OD'd at a party. The people she was with freaked—they were all afraid of getting busted—so they took her outside and left her behind some bushes. And called me on my cell."

"Why?"

"Because they knew I'd come. Because I've done it before. Too many times to count."

Except for a siren in the distance, it was dead quiet. "That's it?" Anna finally asked. "That's your story?"

"I had to go, Anna. As it was, I barely got her to the hospital in time. She was turning blue. "

"I bet."

"Come on. She had convulsions and puked all over my car. There was nothing going on between us."

"I see. So you left me all alone on your father's boat to go get the car. Then you got this call on your cell and you just left. Oh, well, so what if Anna is on my father's boat? No problem, I'll just leave her there, alone and abandoned, in the middle of the night. *That's* your story?"

"You have to understand, the people who called me were crying and screaming. They thought she was dying. It scared the hell out of them. And me."

"Even if I believed you, it wouldn't explain why you didn't call me on the way there."

"I did. Twice. From my car. You didn't answer."

"Ben, you never—" And then Anna remembered. She'd fallen asleep on the boat. Could easily have slept right through her cell phone ringing. "You didn't leave a message. Or call me later on, even."

"What kind of message could I leave? I kept thinking I'd just try you again, but then once I found my friend, all I could think about was saving her. Plus I would have had to be cryptic about her identity, which would have made any message I left even weirder. And then, by the time I was done with her, I figured you'd be so pissed off that you'd never want to hear from me again. I even told my parents not to say where I was."

"You were right. That I wouldn't want to hear from you again."

"Anna." His large hand encircled her slender wrist. "I can't stop thinking about you. I couldn't go back to Princeton without seeing you. We can't just end it like this."

"Who writes your lines, Ben?"

He dropped her wrist and looked as if she'd slapped him. "What?"

She could tell she'd hurt him and in a rush wanted to take it back. But she forced herself to be strong. "Because this story sounds like bad dialogue from a trashy novel."

He held his palms up to her. "It's the truth."

She wouldn't let her eyes meet his. She knew if she did, she'd be lost. So she focused on his chest . . . and remembered what it had felt like to rest her own head there. So warm. So comforting. Damn.

"No, here's the truth, Ben. We had one date. I met some of your friends, and for the most part they weren't the kind of people I'd choose to be with. We went to a party and you disappeared for most of it. We went out on your father's boat, and when I wouldn't have sex with you, you just . . . you dumped me." She could feel an ache behind her eyes but willed herself not to cry.

"Is that what you think?" Ben asked hoarsely. "You think I took off because you wouldn't put out?"

"I'm looking at the facts."

"I wasn't looking for a one-night thing with you, Anna. You've made it pretty clear you're not that kind of girl."

"And you've made it pretty clear that you're that kind of guy. Did you sleep with Dee?"

Ben looked stunned. "What?"

She hadn't meant to bring it up, but there it was. So she asked again. "Did you have sex with Dee?"

"Is that relevant?"

"It's a simple yes-or-no question."

He took a long time before he answered and exhaled deeply. "Once. I think."

"You *think?*"

"She was visiting Princeton. I'd just had a bang-up fight with my dad and I got wasted. The next thing I knew, it was morning and I had the world's worst hangover. Dee was in bed with me."

"You mean you don't remember?"

"No, I don't. Dee keeps calling me, e-mailing me, writing me letters, sending me presents. She says we had sex. Hard to believe, considering how wasted I was."

Anna couldn't bring herself to tell him that Dee claimed to be pregnant with his baby. If Ben was going to get that information, it would have to come from Dee herself.

"Look, I screwed up, Anna."

"With Dee or with me?"

"Forget Dee for a minute. I'm not asking you to forgive me. I know what I did to you was unforgivable. I'm just asking for a chance to make it up to you."

"Why?" she whispered.

"You know why."

Her head was spinning. She wanted to believe him, wanted his story to make sense. But some mystery celebrity OD'ing in the middle of the night who needed Ben and only Ben to come to her rescue? Could that possibly be it? She stared into his eyes, searching for the truth.

"Anna." His hand went to her hair. "Do you know how badly I want to kiss you right now?"

Anna wanted that, too. She did. She wanted to do everything she'd ever imagined in her darkest and wildest fantasies. His lips were so close to hers. It was dangerous to be near him. Yes, she'd come to Los Angeles to reinvent herself. To stop being the cautious, thoughtful girl who lived in her head instead of her heart. But then the worst thing had happened. She'd lost her heart to a boy—*this* boy—and she was pretty damn sure he didn't deserve to have it. What he'd done still hurt. It hurt so much.

She hated feeling this way. Hated, hated, hated it. Where was her dignity, her pride? Who was this shell of a girl she was turning into?

"Anna?" His sad eyes held the question. The decision was in her hands. At that moment she recalled something Cyn had once told her—that it was so much easier when you didn't give a damn. Then you could do anything and everything on your terms, without getting hurt. You were in control. Not him. You.

That's the kind of girl I want to be, Anna thought. Forget love and happy endings—I'll settle for being in control. If anyone does the leaving, it should be me.

She shook her head. "It's too late, Ben. I'd say I'm sorry, but I'm not. You're the one who should be sorry."

"But I am!"

"Save it for the next girl. And treat her better than you treated me."

She turned on her heel and headed back toward school. Ben called to her, but she didn't look back. The more distance she put between herself and him, the stronger she felt. There was a whole world out there waiting for her— all she had to do was reach out and grab it.

Ten feet inside the front door of the school, her cell phone rang again. Without looking, she took the phone from her purse and chucked it into the nearest garbage bin. But the impact of the fall must have tripped the ring tone setting because suddenly her phone was playing "Hava Nagilah." Of all songs! Was this some kind of joke? Some kind of cosmic sound track devised to underscore the absurdity of Anna's situation? The way those five monotonous notes droned over and over—it reminded her of those uncomfortable bar mitzvahs she'd gone to, where the boys and girls stood on separate sides of the room while the hired "dance motivators" tried to force them into pairs and to *party!*

But as Anna walked farther away from the bin and the notes to "Hava Nagilah" grew more faint, it slowly dawned on her that she was missing the point. The ridiculously tacky song was actually delivering an important message—that even though Anna had just had her heart shattered, and even though she had to fight the urge to hop on the next plane for New York, it was all happening on her terms. In essence, it *was* time to party.

Because for once, Anna Cabot Percy was free.